Readers praise ___ ___ Alex Kane novel, *Sweet Dreams*:

"If a book can be judged by how quickly you turn the pages, *Sweet Dreams* is a winner. You may not agree with Kane's methods, but you can't quarrel with his sense of purpose. After such an auspicious debut, the future bodes well for Alex Kane and his creator."
—David K. Krohne
Washington *Blade*

"The only problem with *Sweet Dreams* is that I can't wait to read the next one. I haven't read such a highly-charged entertaining gay fiction in a long time, and I'm truly dying to find out what, or who, Alex Kane is going to avenge next. So hurry up, John Preston, and write!"
—Paul Reed
Bay Area Reporter

"The first of what is to be a series on the adventures of gay avenger Alex Kane is both fun to read and uplifting. Any culture needs richness of mythos in order to grow. Preston's story is a step toward filling a deep need for gay dreams."
— Geoff Mains
The Advocate

"Ultimately I feel that *Sweet Dreams* will prove to be an important contribution to the gay literature of the 1980s. I have high hopes for this series; I wonder if Hollywood will ever discover it."
—T.R. Witomski
The *Connection*

DEADLY LIES

by John Preston

Boston: Alyson Publications, Inc.

Copyright © 1985 by John Preston. All rights reserved.
Cover copyright © 1985 by Gordon Fiedor.

This is a paperback original from Alyson Publications, Inc.,
PO Box 2783, Boston, MA 02208.
Distributed in England by Gay Men's Press,
PO Box 247, London, N15 6RW.

First edition, March 1985   5 4 3 2 1

ISBN 0 932870 66 X

All characters in this book are fictitious.
Any resemblance to real persons, living or dead,
is strictly coincidental.

No, no, I can't swim!
Charles Howard's last words.

On July 7, 1984, after this novel was begun, a young man was thrown from a bridge in Bangor, Maine. He had been beaten by three teen-aged men for only one reason: He was gay. Charles Howard died, drowned in the Kenduskeag Stream. His assailants, tried as juveniles on the reduced charge of manslaughter will spend as little as forty-one months in a juvenile detention center.

The fantasies of Alex Kane, the escapism into the story of a gay vigilante, may be fun entertainment, but they shouldn't allow us to overlook the real world, the world where there must be constant struggle for gay rights and a concrete affirmation of gay dignity.

The University of Southern Maine has instituted a memorial scholarship fund in the memory of Charles Howard. The annual award will go to that student who presents the best essay in defense of gay and lesbian rights. You can make sure that the award has meaning by contributing to it. Your checks, made out to the Charles Howard Memorial Scholarship Fund, should be sent to:

Gay People's Alliance of the
University of Southern Maine
92 Bedford Street
Portland, Maine 04102

I

"I don't like it," Mike Ahern said.

"What don't you like?" Tim Ranson looked over to his co-pilot with hardly any interest. Tim had learned long ago that Ahern was one big bellyache. Here they had one of the most plush jobs in private aviation, and Ahern was always carrying on as though they were slaving in salt mines.

"Having that guy in the plane.

That guy! Tim had recognized the man who was their only passenger. Not that he could ever have forgotten anyone who looked like that. Those green eyes had been so striking that anyone would have to remember them after even the briefest encounter.

Tim had had more than a few jobs piloting the man. He had often wanted to reach out and touch him, just touch him. Partly to see if he was real — there was something about the sharp facial features and the obvious musculature that made the guy look as though he were a Greek statue brought to life by some forgotten ancient god. There was also something obviously sexual about the man — something that Tim couldn't have denied, even if he had wanted to.

"Nothing wrong with him. The job order said pick him up in Chicago and take him to Boston. What's your beef? We're even getting some overtime out of it." Getting overtime on top of their regular salary from Farmdale Industries was no small consideration.

"Someone like that shouldn't be in the old man's seat, that's all." Ahern's jaw was set with his bravado determination. He was playing his usual game, the one that went: *You should know what I'm thinking. You figure it out.*

Normally Tim would ignore the whole thing. He'd gotten pretty good at ignoring Ahern over the last six months they'd been working together. But the subject of the man in the back of the plane was one he had more interest in than usual.

"Look, I don't know what you mean. He's obviously a friend of Farmdale's. I've ferried him around before, so have the other pilots in the fleet. So you might as well get used to it."

"I'll never get used to piloting a faggot." Ahern spat out the words.

So, that was it. Tim's grasp on the controls tightened and he looked down to see the skin around his knuckles turn white with exertion. He was so fucking tired of this game. Damn Ralph and his fucking closet!

Tim relaxed, forcing himself to take a deep breath and get a hold of himself. He glanced one more time at Ahern who seemed to have been satisfied to get his bigoted words out and into the air. Did he know? Did Ahern know that Tim was gay? Was this just a way to needle the pilot he had to work with? Or was it possible he was really that ignorant?

The 727 kept on its course to Boston. Damn Ralph! Tim had to smile though. His lover, Ralph, was the most important person in his life. Tim could picture him walking into their bedroom straight from work, still in his conservative business suit but undressing as quickly as possible so he could join Tim in their big double bed and begin their passionate lovemaking.

He felt a constriction in his underwear just at the

thought of it. His whole life was built around Ralph. Their sex was a part of it, but other things came with it. They enjoyed life together, had a fine apartment, good friends, wonderful vacations . . . and an airtight closet.

Ralph was a lawyer with one of the prestigious firms in downtown Minneapolis, the same city where Farmdale Industries kept its fleet of corporate planes in order to take advantage of the Twin Cities' central location. Ralph was constantly concerned that the other partners in his law firm would discover his sexuality and that they would ruin his career if they did ever find out about him and Tim. They had to go through complicated charades because of Ralph's paranoia.

Some things were just ridiculous. Ralph would mess up Tim's bed before the maid came three times a week to clean. He would insist that they brag about their conquests of women whenever they were around any of Ralph's attorney friends. They even had to rehearse their stories before Ralph would dare to venture out in public. They couldn't go to gay bars in Minneapolis together; only in other cities when they were on vacation would Ralph dare to enter one of those "forbidden places." Nor could they ever have any but the straightest looking friends in their apartment. Ralph was too concerned that a nosy neighbor might happen to pass someone he deemed "too blatant" in the corridor and report him to some kind of imagined thought police.

Usually Tim could handle it all. If it was the price he had to pay for the relationship then it was worth it. But there were so many moments like this one where he had to listen to an idiot like Ahern that made his teeth grind in frustrated anger. There was no avoiding another fact: Those moments were increasing.

Tim just wanted to scream at Ahern: *I'm a cocksucker too!* He wanted to yell: *I get fucked in the ass by my lover and I like it!* At times like this he wanted to march in parades and sing in choruses; he wanted to hold hands in public and live on Castro Street. He was fed up with the bullshit that he had to go through.

But I can't blame Ralph.

Or could he? Ralph was possibly right about losing his job if the partners found out that he was gay. But someone was going to have to do it sometime. Everything was moving, everything was changing., Why couldn't Ralph have the balls to be the first one instead of hiding behind his conservative facade and letting everyone else do all the work and get all the glory?

Tim was sitting at the controls of a Farmdale Industries private jet. It was no surprise that Mike had figured out that the passenger they were carrying was gay. The man was a perfect clone. His leather jacket and his tight jeans, his black leather boots and his white t-shirt, all of it amounted to a uniform. This was someone that the old man knew very well. There had been other hints that Farmdale Industries wasn't going to have any problem hiring a gay man. There were rumors that the oldest son — the one who had died in Vietnam — had been gay. Tim could probably come out in his job and not lose it. He could support Ralph while he built up another career, one that didn't involve hiding and lying about who he was.

Then Tim wouldn't have to be silent in the face of bigots like Ahern. He could just tell him to shut up and be quiet or find another job himself. He could walk down the street with some dignity. He could live without fear and without constant worry that the wrong person was going to walk into the wrong room at the wrong time.

But now, really, he had to be quiet. Silent. He had to sit at the controls and wonder about the man in the back and what kind of life he led. His silence was going to let people like Ahern keep on going, thinking they had more allies than they did.

With immediate regret Tim realized he was helping people like Ahern. For a moment, he realized he was as guilty as the rest of them.
Damn Ralph!

II

The 727 was making its final approach to Boston's Logan International Airport. Alex Kane looked out the window at the familiar skyline without any real interest. He just wanted the plane to be on the ground and he wanted to be moving.

He had to find Danny.

There was always an air of sadness around Alex Kane. There had been too much in his life, it seemed, too much to make him sad. There had been James, his first and, until recently, only lover. James had ripped away the shreds of self-deceipt and forced Alex into the self-awareness that he loved other men.

He had met James in Vietnam, during the war, the war that had been so good at destroying so many illusions. Alex Kane and James Farmdale had been passionate lovers once James had completed Alex's initiation. They had been a team — The Lieutenant and His Sergeant everyone had called them. Then James had been murdered by another American for just that reason: The Lieutenant and His Sergeant had gotten too close. The image of the two men in love with one another had been too disgusting for a beer-bellied NCO from North Dakota who took advantage of a firefight to frag James, to shoot him from the back.

That had begun it. When Alex had turned around and

wreaked his revenge on the killer by performing an immediate execution he had commited himself to a life that he could never have foreseen.

He had tried to avoid it. He had tried by drowning himself in the cheap booze and the faceless bodies of San Francisco's Tenderloin district. But it hadn't worked. Even that one day when Alex had woken up and discovered there was no one in his bed and no money in his pocket and no future that he could see, his avoidance was impossible.

While he had lain there thinking, *So this is the end of the line*, his door was broken down and the goons hired by Joseph Farmdale had captured him. Captured him and taken him unconscious to the Farmdale mansion on the coast of California where the father of his lover was waiting, waiting with his orders and his instructions. Alex Kane had perhaps avenged one death with his actions in Vietnam. But vengeance was not complete. Vengeance would never be done so long as gay men remained the underclass, their fights, dreams, and hopes all brutalized by a society that could no more stand their existence than that NCO had been able to stand Alex and James' lives being intertwined with love.

It had begun: The endless campaigns, the countless battles, the ongoing struggle to secure something for gay men against the overwhelming odds. They had trained Alex Kane's body until it approached mechanical perfection. Farmdale had turned his awesome computers into a weapon of their own. They tracked crime figures, social reports and economic analyses in ways that had never been thought of before, ways that saw the patterns of discrimination and oppression in the gay world.

They hadn't worked.

They hadn't worked enough so far as Alex Kane was concerned at this moment of his life. There was no reason for it all to have happened. He was a failure. The Farmdale operation was a sham. It was for no good reason.

The plane touched the runway. He felt the familiar tug of the resisting jet engines roaring as they brought the craft to a slow motion that allowed a turn towards the terminal.

He had to find Danny and beg forgiveness. He had failed.

• • •

As soon as the plane had stopped, the steward had run to the back and had lowered the steps for Kane's exit. He just nodded unsmilingly at the man and waved away his and a ground attendant's offer of help with Alex's bags. There was only one piece of carry-on luggage. He didn't have time to indulge in the luxury that came with riding the Farmdale private jet. Not that he ever would. Alex Kane wasn't one to indulge in much luxury in any place at any time.

He walked quickly into the terminal and found a bank of coin telephones. He punched a number into the set and waited while the connections were made to California. Farmdale himself answered: "Yes."

This was their private line; Kane was the only person in the world who had the number. "What more do you know?"

"Nothing." The voice at the other end was flat, as though Farmdale felt the same desperate sense of failure as Alex.

"Nothing?" It was an unacceptable answer to Alex right now. All those goddamned computers should have been able to tell them something.

"Only the police reports that we had earlier. I've had men on the case in Boston from the beginning. There's nothing more to say. The culprits have been caught. They're in jail. The evidence is clear and they ..."

"Danny? What about Danny?" Alex demanded.

"I know nothing."

Alex Kane slammed down the receiver.

III

Alex Kane had checked into his usual hotel in Copley Square. He didn't really care about the supposed elegance of the place. He was more interested in the fact that the staff knew him, knew not to bother him. A hotel was just a place to sleep and make phone calls to him. Especially this time.

He'd dropped off his bags and made a few inquiries, but none gave him any idea where Danny might be. There was no answer at the college dormitory. His parents hadn't heard from him in days. There were no other friends that Alex knew well enough to ask for information.

As he'd done before, Alex began his search in the city's gay bars. He went from disco to raunch, from LaCoste to leather; none of them gave him the first clue.

At ten o'clock that night he stopped short. He was walking down Cambridge Street on the way to still another bar hoping someone would know something about Danny. But now he had suddenly realized that he knew precisely where he should be looking.

Of course.

He closed his eyes and rubbed a hand over his forehead. That's where Danny would be. He sighed and turned around, walking back towards the Charles River.

There was no need to rush now. Danny would be there.

Danny wouldn't leave there for a while. Alex followed the winding paths along the banks of the Charles until, after passing Massachusetts General Hospital, he came to the approach to the Longfellow Bridge.

The bridge spanned the Charles just over the locks that protected Boston's riverfront from the effects of the ocean tide. A subway line rose up on the same structure, coming up from its underground tunnel to take an easy route over the water. Alex climbed up the sidewalk parallel to the transit line and ignored the loud rumble of the passing cars.

Danny Fortelli stood on the bridge, halfway between Boston and Cambridge. He was staring down at the black water. The lights of Boston and Cambridge reflected off the surface, bright neon against ebony. Danny wasn't noticing any of the special effects of the urban illumination. The expression on his face clearly was concentrating on the darkness; the bottomless appearance of the river seemed to be seducing him.

"Danny?"

The younger man slowly looked up when he heard Alex speak his name. It seemed as though he had expected Alex all along. He just nodded his head without speaking.

Danny Fortelli was a handsome young man. While Alex Kane was someone you always remembered — those eyes, the chisled features and his air of sadness were all memorable characteristics — he was not picture perfect. There were lines that were too hard in his facial features. His appearance was striking and sexual, but didn't have the appeal of a commercial model.

Danny did. His hair was nearly as dark as Alex's and it was more curly. His shoulders were more noticeably wide, the proportions more in line with the ideal of American manhood that Madison Avenue was giving out. His cheeks were dimpled, a slight hint of his boyishness showing through there. His complexion was unflawed. He was a gymnast, and his taunt torso's sleek lines weren't hidden beneath the simple jeans and flannel shirt that he wore.

He was, in fact, the gay man that every gay man dreams about. There might be some idiosyncracy somewhere that would make him unattractive to someone, but that person would have to look awfully hard to find it. Even now, in his obvious mourning, he was beautiful, so handsome that Alex found himself automatically responding to him, even though this obviously wasn't a time or place to act on it.

"I've been looking for you. All over the city. I got here as fast as I could."

Danny nodded once more. He had turned back to study the surface of the Charles again. A tear slipped out of one eye and tracked down his right cheek.

There wasn't any more that Alex could say. He needed some opening, Danny had to say something to give him a clue. Did Danny want to be alone? Did he want to go home? Did he want to go back to the hotel? Alex would have done anything, but he had to know what Danny wanted.

After a few moments of excruciating silence, the other man started to talk. "This is where they did it." His hand moved out over the edge of the bridge, pointing down toward the water. "This is where they threw him out into the river."

Another tear followed the first. Alex watched helplessly as Danny's throat moved with small convulsions, fighting back his sobs.

"He'd never learned how to swim. I was going to teach him this summer. I made him promise he'd go with me to the beach so I could teach him." His battle with the tears was a losing one. They were streaking down Danny's cheek faster now.

"Danny, I . . ." Alex was at a loss. He wanted to touch this man he loved; he didn't dare. He wanted to comfort him; he didn't know how.

"They say they didn't know Sy couldn't swim. They say

it was supposed to be just a prank. The subway was going by. He was screaming, but they thought he was just acting like a queen, just screaming for the sake of screaming, so they went ahead, thinking — they *say* — he'd just get to the shore.

"He didn't. He didn't get two feet. He thrashed around, there were witnesses who saw that, then he went under. He never came up again."

Danny finally looked towards Alex. He had delivered his description of the murder of his best friend with a controlled monotone. But now, looking at Alex's face, no longer able to keep in the pain, he screamed at the top of his lungs.

"*Why?! Why?!*"

Then the sobs were overwhelming. Danny's hands went to cover his face and his knees seemed to buckle underneath him. Alex quickly took the few steps between them and clutched Danny to his own chest, his hands tried to give comfort, his lips softly touched Danny's face.

Through the wails Danny kept on asking, "Why, why, why?"

Anger and grief, fury and sorrow battled inside Alex as he held Danny tightly. Wrath and sorrow fought for his attention. He didn't know which was going to win.

The subway careened up out of its tunnel and passed them, its loud noise momentarily blanketing the noises of Danny's lament. But Alex Kane knew this was an anguish that wouldn't be easily dismissed. This was a desolation that would stay for a long, long time.

IV

Danny was finally asleep on the big bed in Alex's hotel room, his mouth was open, his breath was softly audible adding to an impression of youthfulness. *He's only nineteen years old*, Alex reminded himself. Nineteen years old. It seemed impossible.

Danny had the wisdom of a much older person. It had come to him through his willingness to always listen, to never play-act being older than he was. He went through life absorbing things that people said and observing how they acted. Only when all his information was complete would Danny act.

The wisdom came from other places too. Alex sat on one of the big overstuffed chairs in the room and continued to watch his lover as he thought back to their meeting. Kane had come to Boston after the Farmdale computers had discovered a pattern of personal destruction in the city's young men. There was a cause to anything that devastating, there had to be. It was Kane's job to discover that cause and to eliminate it.

He found the poisoned web that was entrapping some of the best and brightest gay youth in Massachusetts. It had been a blackmail ring. Handsome young men would be seduced by operatives not knowing that their activities were being videotaped and photographed. Then the evidence was used to force them into a vile and erosive prostitution.

Danny had been one of the victims. At the age of eighteen he had been forced to serve up a series of perverse sexual acts to paying customers who dealt with him and the others as oddities. Prostitution itself wasn't such a bad thing, it was often a means of survival for men and for women who had no other economic option. Some of them gave decent human services to decent human beings who needed their companionship. But the use of blackmail was unavoidably negative, its effect was unconscionable.

Alex had broken up the ring through a tip from Sy, Danny's best friend, and a remarkable young man in his own right. Sy was one of the thousands of gay men who had found their freedom on the streets. Viciously abused by his father, Sy had left his home and made his own life, financing his adventure with occasional prostitution. It was his street smarts and his willingness to talk to Alex Kane that had delivered the information necessary to destroy the evil kingpin who had been responsible for the destruction of so many young men — until Alex Kane had sent him flying out of a skyscraper window and into the waiting arms of Storrow Drive.

Sy. Tall, skinny, effeminate, strong Sy. The one who wore his gayness with abandon, who organized street kids and the spark that kept the Gay Youth Discussion Group going. Sy. Vibrant, courageous, dead Sy.

Kane picked up the copy of the Boston *Globe* and read the story for still another time. It seemed so easy to read the cold type of the newspaper. It was so distant.

GAY YOUTH MURDERED BY TOUGHS

Boston Police reported today that Sy Mestrell, 23, of Boston drowned last night when a gang of local youths known as The Angels threw him from the Longfellow Bridge.

Mestrell, originally from Somerville, evidently could not swim. He died only a few hundred feet from the banks of the Charles River.

Indicted for second degree murder in Suffolk County District Court were . . .

Kane put down the paper and closed his eyes. He wouldn't even have the satisfaction of catching the ones who did it. The police had moved in quickly and effectively for once. The gang had been under surveillance for a while. There was an undercover agent in their midst when they'd taken Sy and tossed him into the river. The arrests had been quick, the prosecution was going to be effective.

Not so for Sy, but because the police wanted the group off the streets. Sy was just their excuse. Kane tried to get his anger stoked up over that reality. But he couldn't. He couldn't feel it while he looked at Danny and realized the hurt and loss that Danny Fortelli felt. His best friend was dead. There was nothing anyone could do.

What's the use of this life if I can't even protect my lover from this pain? The thought ravaged Kane's mind. That was the reason he judged himself a failure. For years he'd dedicated himself to this battle against anyone who would dare to attack the vulnerable lives of gay men. James had been the beginning, the beginning of his vow that gay men should live decent lives free from the constant fear of hatred.

He had had some successes. There were young gay men roaming the streets who had never tasted heroin's poison because of Alex Kane's work. There were old gay men who were living in respectful comfort in adequate retirement homes because he had stopped the leeches who would have eaten their savings and their precious last years.

But he couldn't stop Sy from being murdered.
What's the use?

V

The waiter in the hotel restaurant watched the two men as they ate their breakfast. *Why should they look so sad?* he wondered. *If I had one or the other I'd be in heaven.*

His name was Eric Appel. He'd been serving up food to travelers and tourists for five years now. The hotel might be four-star rated in the guide books, but he was just slinging hash so far as he was concerned. It was all just a scam to earn the money to keep up his own quest for the lust of his life, a man he was determined to find in one of Boston's gay bars. His determination was immense. He kept up his search every night of the week, supplementing his constant wanderings with regular visits to a local gym.

He had the looks, he had the pecs and he had the desire. But somehow his goal had always avoided him. He had the right to be sad, not them. *Look at them*, he thought.

The young one was too good looking for words, so attractive Eric wondered if he hadn't seen him in one of the gay magazines. Eric would have killed for hair as naturally thick and curly as that. He could only have been twenty or so, but there was ample evidence that there was a matching rug on the guy's chest, little wiffs of hair were creeping up over his shirt collar. He was the kind of guy who could wear any clothes and all those assets of his would still show up. Eric had watched him when he'd walked in. That was a *significant* ass.

The other one was weird. He was easily ten years older. That didn't faze Eric. Ten years older, ten years younger, his lover-to-be could be either one. The man's eyes were strange. That was where the weirdness came in. They seemed to change in intensity with the man's moods. He'd certainly gone through some moods in a short time this morning. Anger had flashed for a while; so had a look of love that Eric had always wanted to have directed toward himself. It had been an expression of sheer adoration that had come over the guy. Then the sadness had crept in. Deep, deep sadness, like the guy was going to cry.

They must be breaking up, Eric thought. It was the only excuse for that look that he could imagine. *But why would they ever break up?* he questioned. *If you had that in bed every night, how could you leave it?*

He went over and poured coffee in the two half-empty cups, hoping that one or the other man would notice him. If there was a divorce going on here, he was perfectly willing to pick up any pieces that were available. But they ignored him, continuing to study the white linen tablecloth.

Well, maybe they'd be in the bars alone later tonight. Eric wondered which ones they'd go to and revised his schedule to make sure he was present in those he guessed the most likely.

Either one would do me fine, Eric thought.

• • •

Neither Danny or Alex had noticed the waiter. They were startled to discover their coffee cups full. Each grabbed at his cup, glad to have the distraction.

After more painful silence, Alex finally spoke. "What would you like to do?" It seemed a pitiful question. Kane hated this feeling of inadequacy.

Danny seemed to think for a while. "I want to go away."

It was delivered that simply. Alex felt his stomach

tighten. Did that mean Danny wanted to go away from him? Was he going to get thrown out with the rest it?

"Where can we go?"

Alex sighed with relief. "Anywhere you want. Really. Anywhere."

"Away from people. I just want to be alone. I just want to be with you."

"Danny, I don't know if . . ."

"Alex, I just want to go away." Danny had cut Kane off before he had a chance to try to present anything that could masquerade as another option. "I want to get away from all this shit." His hands tightened around his coffee cup. "I don't want to deal with it any more."

"Then we won't, Danny. We don't have to." Kane reached across and massaged one of Danny's hands. "I have plenty of money. More than enough. We'll just go. Wherever you want."

Danny leaned back in his chair and saw the crowds walking busily through Copley Square. "The mountains. It's summer. I don't want to stay in the city in the summer."

"Fine," Alex said quickly. "We'll go to the mountains for the summer. Then you can come back when school starts again . . ."

"I don't know about that, Alex." Danny was still looking out the window. "I don't know what I'm going to do when the summer's over." He sipped more coffee. "I don't want to plan."

"You don't have to." Kane knew he was speaking too quickly. His concern about staying with Danny and somehow soothing the pain his lover felt was too pressing on him. He tried to calm himself. "Is your car here?"

Danny nodded. "Not far, it's in a garage."

"Good, let's get our stuff and check out. We'll just drive north. We'll find something for the night and then look around for something more permanent."

"Permanent . . ." Danny almost whispered the words. He finally looked at Alex. "You want that, don't you, permanent?"

Alex was stunned. "Of course I do. We've talked about that before. I've always wanted something that would last with you."

"No you didn't. You didn't at all in the beginning. You played all kinds of games about it."

"Danny, please. We've been through that. Yeah, it was difficult for me in the beginning. But for the last six months it's been obvious that I want to stay with you, hasn't it?"

Danny nodded. It was hardly a major affirmation, but Alex wasn't going to argue about it. Danny went back staring out the window and Alex realized suddenly that he had that same expression as he had last night, when he was looking down into the black water of the Charles, studying Sy's grave. A chill went through Alex's body. *Permanent.* Was Danny worrying about Alex meeting the same fate? Was that the problem? Was he afraid he would find love only to have it snatched away?

It had happened to Alex Kane when James had died. He could never be the cause of it happening to Danny Fortelli. But what else could Danny be thinking of? Look at the life Alex led, the constant danger, the seeking out of possibly mortal battles.

Permanent.

At least with reason, Alex supposed. Why shouldn't Danny want that? Why shouldn't Danny have that? If all of Alex Kane's struggles abandoned Danny this way, what was the use? None.

Alex Kane was making some decisions that he didn't dare investigate.

VI

"What's the use of all this bullshit I've been doing?!" State Representative Andrew Marston threw his sheaf of paper down on the big conference table that dominated the meeting room. Around it sat his campaign advisers. "You assholes have told me for years that I had to get a good record going. So I did it. I did all the crap you wanted me to do.

"I should have divorced the alcoholic bitch you call my wife ten years ago. But, oh no, you said I had to have the image of a good family man. So I kept her. You've made me go to feminist meetings with a bunch of dykes who'd like to cut off my pecker, you've forced me to march in gay pride parades, you made me go against every value I hold and act as though I love and support fucking labor unions, you . . ."

"It was the right thing to do," insisted Marty O'Brien, Marston's top aide.

"The right thing to do isn't going to get me elected dogcatcher in Minnesota any more." Marston was furious and disgusted. He picked up the papers once more and flipped through them. But the figures weren't going to change and the conclusions weren't going to alter. "The damn thing's all for shit. All of it. The field's so crowded with left-wing candidates now that there's no way in hell I'm going to get the governor's seat."

"Who could have anticipated the change in the electorate? Minnesota was supposed to be the most liberal state in the country. Anyone looking at your chances ten years ago would have told you what we all did — establish yourself on the left. Things changed in ways that we could never have thought. Abortion, national pride, stupid mistakes by other Democrats, all of it was unforeseeable." O'Brien was getting red in the face as he defended the counsel he'd given Marston.

But the would-be candidate wasn't buying any. "For Christ's sake, the field of liberal candidates is overcrowded. We're all going to knock each other off, spend huge amounts of money doing it, and then whoever is unlucky enough to win is going to get the shit beaten out of him by the Republicans. It's clear as day.

"These last ten years have been wasted, absolutely wasted. The master plan is a farce. We're all going to look like assholes."

No one could argue with Marston. He was speaking the obvious truth, and they all knew it. There he was, tall, thick-haired, perfect teeth and an athletic body, the perfect candidate. He had the right background: good middle-class family, football star in college, law school, never a hint of scandal in his personal or his public life.

That last part was important, because the group that sat around the table where he was presiding sure did have more than a few scandals among them.

Marty O'Brien was the cleanest, but that was only because he had never been caught. O'Brien was from the old school of politics. He knew every dirty trick in the books. He knew how to get people who had been dead for fifteen years to vote for his candidates. He knew which ballot boxes could be bought for how much in which precincts. He had a dossier on every major and minor political figure in the state that told him where the mistresses were hidden, how the illegal money was kept away from inquiring eyes, and just when which politician had been caught drunk driving in what state. He was the perfect campaign manager for Andrew Marston. He had no morals and he wouldn't even know what they looked like if he happened to find some wandering around in his soul. He only knew how to win.

Not winning was going to be much more of a bother to Luther Angstrom. The head of the Minneapolis drug trade had to have a man he could trust in the governor's mansion. He'd invested millions of dollars in Marston. If it didn't produce the desired result then there were some very painful investigations going on in the state police department that could have even more painful results for him. He studied Marston and O'Brien carefully, picking at his nails with a letter opener. No one had to say the obvious: Something awfully similar to that letter opener could be used to pay back anyone that Angstrom thought was doing him wrong.

Angstrom usually did make sure he collected on those kinds of debts. He'd learned the hard way that being tough was the only way to succeed in his business. It was a lucrative operation, so lucrative that some guys down in Chicago had once thought it might be a good thing to move in on it. The result had been one of the bloodiest gang wars in recent history, one that left dead bodies of Angstrom's friends and foes all over the corn and wheat fields that surrounded Minneapolis. Once he'd been blooded and seen the good effect that the sight of a dead man can have, Angstrom was like a wild animal who'd been unleashed for the first time.

Martin Martello was one of the only men at the table who wasn't too concerned with the implied threat of Angstrom's paper opener. He had his own scam, one more than successful enough to keep him from coveting the other gangster's. Martello ran one of the largest and most profitable prostitution rings in the country. It was national in scope. He moved women around with the efficiency of Avis or Hertz. Need more product in Florida during the winter? Charter a plane and ship your surplus from the Northeast down to where the demand was. Was Atlantic City low on stock? There was extra inventory in Buffalo. Hire a bus and right the balance.

Martello even had computers working on those problems. But so did the FBI have computers working on the problem that was Martin Martello. And if those computers kept on getting helpful hints from the Minnesota Attorney General's office, Martello was going to discover himself as the prize in one hell of a big bingo game.

The rest of the group had similar investments in Marston's long march to the governor's office. They were desperate for his victory and just as desperately opposed to any other man or woman sitting in that chair.

But they had all taken part in the miscalculation. It had sounded so good, so obvious. In a liberal state, elect a liberal man. Take over the state government and use it like real men had used it in the past. They all had dreams of a return to the days of politicians who had understood the value of a dollar — at least a dollar that had been deposited in a secret bank account.

When the left wing of the Democratic Party had begun to take over they had all been caught in a wave of self-righteous crusading that was led by people who didn't give a damn about their own private wealth and who were too happy to subvert the time-honored way things were done.

The only option seemed to be to co-opt that movement. That's when they'd set up Marston. He had been well on his way to victory when the electorate had taken a sharp turn to the right. Law and order was the big issue now. Abortion undercut much of the feminist movement's appeal to middle-class women who had once been their major support. Gay rights had turned off many of the religious moderates. Unions were getting a worse name and their membership was drastically declining.

And they were stuck with Marston.

Andrew Marston looked over the room and studied the faces of the men who were sitting in wait for some answer. He knew perfectly well what was going through their minds. He was a liability now. A nothing so far as they were concerned. His access to their funds and their resources was about to be cut off and with it would go his dreams of ultimate power.

They thought they were going to use him once he's gotten to the governor's mansion. They were wrong. Once he was there his plan had always been to turn the tables on them. They were stuck in old-fashioned modes. Oh, Martello may have finally discovered the values of computers, but he was an exception. These men were stereotypes of old-fashioned gangsters.

They held their fiefs through sheer brute force. What they didn't realize was that if the power of the state was really directed toward them, directed by someone like himself who understood just how they worked, they would all be knocked off in a matter of days.

If he could grasp hold of the sophisticated resources of the Minnesota State Police and direct it at organized crime, he could wipe it out in a matter of days. But, of course, he didn't intend for the crimes to be destroyed, just these kingpins. Use him? He was going to use them. Nature abhors a vacuum; remove the natural parasites who lived off people's vices and you only created the situation where a new parasite would thrive. And the next one was going to be named Andrew Marston.

If he could ever get to the governor's mansion, that was.

"So we change priorities," O'Brien said.

"After ten years I'm supposed to stop loving Teddy Kennedy and start wanting to stand proud with the John Birch Society? Don't you think that's a little much for people to swallow? We've invested everything to make me look like the good clean, conscientious citizen. How can I justify the turnabout?"

Angstrom was cleaning his fingernails still. He stopped and looked up at Marston. "So find a reason to change that people can buy."

Marston stopped short for a moment. A change that people can buy? If it existed, it should be right here in this room. The men here represented everything that an honest person would hate. Violence, drugs, prostitution, illegal gambling . . .

No, no, he thought, *they're too expected*. You can't start a crusade against something that people expect. Nor could you suddenly turn around on an issue like abortion. It was too tricky, there was as much support for it as there was feeling against it. Then what? What would get people so pissed off that they would understand a candidate . . .

"Fags!" Andrew Marston shouted. "Everyone hates fags! What if the faggots in Minnesota started to do things that got everyone really upset, really angry and disgusted. What if I was the one who started the movement against them? I could do that with the radio program.

"I could introduce bills in the state legislature. I could begin a new crusade!" Marston's eyes were glassy with the thought.

Martin Martello, Luther Angstrom and the rest of the crew went through their mental files. Martello was the first to draw the obvious conclusion: "They don't do anything that other people don't do." Martello had once been amazed at some of the specific sexual acts his clientele requested from his women. But that had been a long time ago, so long ago that now he was incapable of responding to any sexual preference with anything but a yawn.

"But we can make them do things that will shock the hell out of the public." Marston was on a roll now. He had his answer. "Think of everything that the suburban mother thinks fags might do. Think of every possible thing that would turn a liberal minister's stomach, make an ACLU lawyer throw up. Think! Think! Think! We'll stage it all."

Martello was the first to sit up in his chair. Sure, he was used to anything on the possible menu, but if his wife knew what . . . "It could work."

"We'll make it work," Marston insisted.

"How?" Angstrom stopped picking at his nails. This was getting interesting.

"Sure, fags do lots of things in private that would upset people. But it's all hushed up. Well, we just make sure it gets very public and very messy. You guys must be able to help me on this. You know what's going on here in the city and in St. Paul."

"Sure, there's leather stuff, and some guys like teenagers," Martello admitted. He'd gotten some requests from clients that proved that.

"Okay, there's the start. Leather. People hate that. What if it turned really dangerous and really dirty? I mean, what if it got *sick!*"

"They play games," Martello swept his arms open. "Big deal."

"What if their games got out of hand? Say their games got real bloody."

Martello looked on with interest. "Yeah, I mean, you take risks, sometimes you fall on your face."

"And those guys that like boys . . . "

"No big deal," Martello dismissed that idea. "Look, you want a young piece of skirt, there's skirt out there waiting for you. You want it with a pecker, it's there too."

"But if it was violent? If there was evidence that it was organized? If it was something that we could smear all over the papers? Come on, come on, don't you see? We'll create reality from the public's worst fantasies. It's perfect. It's fucking perfect.

"I can even make it so some of the fags come over to us. You know the type, the ones that want to be married in churches and have you think they're just like real men. Well, we'll make it look like there's someone attacking the gays. We'll make it so bad we'll get them to lead the crusade to close the gay bars."

"Hold it a minute!" Sonny LeBec wasn't buying any of that. He'd been silent during the whole meeting. But Sonny's many holdings included a couple of very lucrative gay bars. He didn't want to give those up.

"For the short run. Of course the bars will open up again. There'll always be places for the fags to meet."

"We'll make it up to you, Sonny." Angstrom had put away his letter opener. "Let's talk some specifics. I think our boy here has an answer to our problems."

Andrew Marston broke into a big grin. He was going to have another chance to win.

VII

Alex Kane tried to let his senses take over. If he could only just let the bright, warm sun and the cool water overwhelm his thoughts, then, perhaps, they could be shut off.

He was on a float in the middle of a small, isolated lake in the White Mountains of New Hampshire. He was naked, there were no people around. The sunlight that was heating his skin was erotic. *Think about that,* Alex commanded himself.

His legs were spread far apart, each one hanging over a side of the plastic float. The water was just able to reach his testicles as they hung down. It was also cooling his buttocks. *Think about that,* he said to himself again. This time he smiled.

He could still feel the afterglow of his sex with Danny there, between his legs. The younger man had gone at it with abandon last night and again this morning. He was driven with sexuality it seemed. Maybe he was using it to escape . . .

Don't think about that.

Sex with Danny, just think about sex with Danny. The smile returned. For years Alex Kane had only used sex as another one of his tools. It was something he used to barter with, to gain entrance to closed circles or to collect information. Very occasionaly he used it as a form of recreation. When he had found another man who was as independent and as anxious to avoid emotional entanglements as he had been, then Alex could jump into the arena of recreational sex.

But from the beginning, sex had been different with Danny. Alex sometimes felt as though Danny had a strange power of his own, one that he could use to rip through Alex's defenses. The intense physical training that Kane had gone through had had a side effect. He had become a sexual athlete, one who could provoke the most intense and almost spiritual reactions from his partners. Over and over again men would stop in the middle of sex and ask him, "How did you do that?" He would only reply, "It's just something you learn."

It had been that to him, just something that he had learned. Something you did to achieve an orgasm. He had never had any kind of relationship with another man after James Farmdale, perhaps because he couldn't imagine suffering that kind of loss again. Perhaps . . .

But Danny had made him lose it all. From the beginning, sex with Danny had been disarming. Alex couldn't use his skills against him. They were useless. Danny made Alex respond like an overanxious teenager himself. He longed for the feel of Danny's skin, he dreamed of his mouth covering Danny's cock, the same cock he loved to have driven inside him.

Now his face was breaking into a huge smile. His buttock muscles tensed as he thought of Danny fucking him. The guy had been a gymnast when Alex had met him. His torso was a perfect sight, covered with a soft pelt of dark body hair. His stomach was chiseled, his thighs tight as most men's biceps. And when he decided to fuck, he used all his own physical expertise to drive his body into Alex's.

Alex almost never got fucked. At least, he hadn't until Danny came along two years ago. But it was the guy's preference and Alex certainly wasn't going to deny him. Usually when Alex met a man the other male would assume that Kane was going to be "on top." It was the harsh way he came on, he supposed; he knew his appearance was one that fed a lot of people's fantasies about a "real man."

So Alex had gotten used to doing the fucking. Then comes Danny and he wants the situation reversed. It had taken Kane a little bit to get used to the idea, but once he did, he wasn't in any mood to argue.

His cock was ramrod hard now, bouncing off his belly as it jerked with the thoughts of his excitement. Alex rolled over; he liked the feel of the cool lake water on his erection, and he rubbed it slightly against the plastic. He couldn't help but think of masturbating this way. The pleasure was consuming him.

"That was a mistake."

Alex turned and looked over his shoulder towards the shore. There was Danny, his body also naked, his hands playing with his naked crotch. They were only a couple hundred feet apart. Their mutual admiration didn't have much distance to hide it.

"Why mistake?" Alex teased.

"It was going to be fun to watch you get hard, but I can't hold back if you're going to show off your ass that way."

"Don't you have any self-discipline?"

"Not where that's concerned."

"Well, what are you going to do about it? If you think I'm going to just swim in every time you throw a boner, you're crazy."

"Then I'll have to come and get you."

Danny stretched his arms over his head and leapt into the water and swam right over to the plastic raft. Alex was able to turn back over before Danny got to him. The young man grabbed the raft and half climbed up it, right at the apex of Alex's legs. He smiled, then pulled on the legs, bringing Alex toward him and his waiting mouth.

Alex moaned as Danny took in his erection and used his tongue to send sensations from the tip of Alex's cock to the furthest extremes of his body. An unwilling groan of pleasure escaped from Alex's mouth.

Danny stopped suddenly. He smiled at his lover. "Well, do you want to come back up to the cottage where we could get a little more . . . sophisticated?"

"I didn't think you were that big on sophistication," Alex responded.

"I'm a good learner. I have a good teacher." Danny reached up and cupped Alex's testicles in one palm. "Quick and easy right here, or long and slow up there?"

"Up there." Alex slipped off the float and the two men swam back to the shore.

• • •

Even though it was June, this part of New Hampshire was high in the mountains and the evenings still had enough crispness to justify a fire. Alex watched the flames grow in the stone hearth. They were mesmerizing. That was good; it meant another thing to take his mind away from his thoughts.

Not that Danny wasn't doing a good job of that.

They were on the floor, their bodies sprawled on the thick carpet. Danny seemed to be napping. He deserved it. He'd worked hard all day, hard at staying hard. When Danny had offered "long and slow" he'd meant just that. Long and slow for hours.

The opening between Alex's legs wasn't just warm now, it was heated, even a little raw from the use Danny had given it. *Time to do a little role-switching*, Alex thought. That wasn't going to be any problem. He could see the twin mounds of hair-covered muscles right now. Danny was lying on his stomach, his head on Alex's chest. It would be a pleasure to do nothing but switch roles back and forth. Fuck, get fucked. Suck, get sucked. With Danny, it would be pure bliss, in fact.

All we need is one another, Alex thought. *We could be so happy with just one another.*

VIII

Tim Ranson was tired. He'd just finished a long flight, a round trip from Minneapolis to Kansas City with a big layover. He was sitting in the cab, grateful not to have to drive his own car home. The taxi was speeding up Interstate 35 toward downtown.

Tim had a copy of the *Minneapolis Tribune* in his hands. However fatigued he might have been, the headlines in the paper were enough to wake him up.

GAY SEX RING UNCOVERED

What the hell was going on that a liberal paper like the *Tribune* was leading with that kind of scare? It wasn't like the newspaper to feed lines of yellow journalism to the public.

But the story answered the question clearly enough.

> Minneapolis Police, following an anonymous tip, discovered today that a ring of professional men, all evidently homosexual, have been involved in the buying and selling of young immigrant boys.
>
> The youths, who police say were imported from various Caribbean countries, were all between the ages of fourteen and seventeen. They were kept in virtual slavery by their supposed employers who threatened them with arrest and extradition if their sexual demands weren't fulfilled . . .

The story went on. The *Tribune* was a family newspaper and didn't pander to lust-hungry readers with unnecessary gory details. But Tim could read between the lines. The kids had been recruited in poverty-stricken villages, promised a decent life and, instead, discovered themselves misused and maltreated by a set of middle-class gays.

The story sickened Tim. He read carefully over the list of men implicated in the scheme. A doctor, a couple of engineers, a dentist whose name was familiar to Tim, it must have been someone Tim had met. Allen Chisle. He thought for a while. Allen Chisle. Hell, the guy had been at the same Christmas party as Tim and Ralph.

Tim stared out the window and watched the freeway traffic speed by. Who would ever have guessed that Chisle was someone who would have been caught up in a scam like that? He had seemed a really nice guy, interested in Tim and his career. He's been interested in more than that until Tim had made it clear he had a lover. Allen had even seemed to respect the fact of the relationship.

Tim had liked the man a great deal. He had even played with the fantasy that Chisle would certainly be a great candidate for an affair if Tim was ever going to take up something on the side.

But that hadn't gone far. Ralph was adamant about their monogamy and Tim respected his lover's wishes. But how could Tim have been so far off about Allen? If someone was going to be so clearly interested in a 35-year old man like Tim, how could he go off the deep end and wind up treating a young boy like a piece of chattel?

The cab driver turned off the freeway and wound the car through the streets of Minneapolis. Tim and Ralph lived in a highrise on the banks of the Mississippi River which bisected the city. By the time the driver had pulled up to the entrance, Tim had nearly forgotten about Allen Chisle's indiscretions. So he had made a miscalculation? It was just further proof that it wouldn't be a good idea for him to play around on Ralph. Jesus, he could have been caught up in that mess himself.

Tim paid the driver and dragged his bag from the back seat of the taxi. He nodded to the doorman as he entered the imposing lobby of his building. He whistled softly as he waited for the elevator to arrive. He was smiling when it did. Ralph would be waiting. It was late, too late for dinner. But not too late for sex.

The elevator seemed to take forever to rise up to the fifteenth floor where the two men had their apartment. Tim walked swiftly down the corridor to their door and opened it with his key. He was still whistling when he walked in and heard the music.

It was a Bach fugue, something Ralph usually wouldn't have had playing. Tim didn't think much about it. There was a strange smell though, as though Ralph had burnt a late dinner. In fact, it stank. Tim called out. "Hey, Ralph, where are you?" He didn't get a reply. He walked into the bedroom, wondering if Ralph was planning a surprise for him.

There was a surprise, all right, but it wasn't one that Ralph had planned. Someone else had done the honors. There, spreadeagled on their bed, was Tim's lover. He was dead. He had to be. His genitals weren't attached to his torso. They were cut off, on the ground at the foot of the bed. Where they had been was only a gaping hole — a hole where nearly all of Ralph's blood had spilled out.

Tim didn't have time to think. He stood straight up as he vomited.

• • •

Tim felt as though it was all some bad dream, some horrible joke that had been played on him. All around him the police and their technicians thronged, picking through the evidence. Unbelieving, he watched as two men from the coroner's office carried out a large plastic bag that Tim knew contained his lover's body.

"Mr. Ranson, I'm afraid I have to talk to you."

Tim looked up and tried to remember the name of the

police detective. Carlson, that was it, Lieutenant Carlson from the homicide division.

"Yeah, of course. Can I get you some coffee?" What a ludricous thing to ask. Coffee during a murder investigation.

"No thank you." The officer didn't seem to think Tim's reaction was strange. He sat down on a sofa across from Tim's chair. "We know you were in Kansas City tonight. We know what time your plane returned to the airport."

Of course, Tim thought, *I would be a suspect.*

"So, obviously, since the time of death was determined as about six this evening, you are totally in the clear." Carlson must have been through this many times, but he still seemed uncomfortable delivering the judgment to Tim. He averted his eyes for a moment, as though he felt guilty even thinking that Tim would have murdered Ralph . . . especially that way.

Tim just nodded.

"Can you give us any idea about your . . . roommate's friends?"

"He wasn't just my roommate, he was my lover." Tim felt some strange and great relief to finally be able to say that. It was a minor victory in the middle of all the rest, but it still felt god-damned good. *My lover* . . .

"I . . . assumed so. I still have to ask about his other friends."

Tim hesitated. "Mainly people from his office. He worked at a firm here in Minneapolis." The detective nodded, indicating he already had that information. "Then, well, a few friends of mine knew him." Tim rattled off the short list of gay men that he and Ralph used to see. *Used to see* . . .

"Do you know," Carlson stopped short for a moment. Then he began again, apparently forcing himself to go through with this unpleasant conversation. "Do you know if any of them were also interested in the kinks that your friend enjoyed?"

"My *friend* didn't enjoy any kinks." Tim sat up straight. He stared into the policeman's eyes. "My *friend* never got into any kink at all." It was true. Ralph had been a good lover and a hot bed partner, but he had been straight vanilla for the years he and Tim had lived together.

The way Carlson reacted infuriated Tim further. The detective obviously didn't believe Tim's judgment. "Well, but perhaps some of his other gay friends were . . . inclined that way. Maybe they experimented every so often with one another."

"They did not." Tim would know. If there was any experimenting to be done, he would have done it. He was always vaguely interested, Ralph had always rebuffed his hints with a trace of disgust.

"Mr. Ranson, someone entered this apartment with your friend's permission. There's no sign of forced entry. He tied your friend to the bed. There's no sign of a struggle. Your friend enjoyed — or endured — at least an hour's worth of physical activity from our reports. There's no sign of drugs to indicate any unfair play. Then your friend's companion went too far. Obviously, he went way too far. Now, we're grown ups in the police department, Mr. Ranson. I'm not going to make any moral judgments about what activities you and the rest of you take part in. But I have some experience in these things and I knowed damned well that what went on in that bedroom wasn't in any way a little experimentation. Those men knew what they were doing, they did it with finesse and knowledge . . . up to the end.

"Mr. Ranson, your pal was no amateur. He was playing in the big leagues. I want to know all about his activities. I want to know where he learned his lessons."

Carlson sat there waiting. Tim couldn't help but cry. He covered his face with his hand. "I honest to god don't know."

IX

Joseph Farmdale knew that he should be impressed with the New England countryside that sped by his car window. His rented limousine was climbing up the White Mountains. There was still snow occasionally visible on the top of Mt. Washington. That, his memory reminded him, was not unusual. It was still June.

He sighed at the labor involved in trying to find comfort in things aesthetically pleasing. It wasn't his forte. Farmdale had truly given up that direction of life's pleasures decades ago. His were now found in the maintenance of what he called a sense of propriety. He did enjoy the results of good breeding, the kind he could see clearly in his thoroughbred horses back on his California ranch. He only wished that good breeding had shown in his children. It had, actually, and the evidence of it in his first son, James, had been the greatest pleasure of his life, for as long as that pleasure lasted. But the other illustrations of breeding in his own family line had been just as distinctly disappointing.

Farmdale sneered at the remembrance of the rest of his children. James had been such a Farmdale! He had had the dignity and the intelligence that good breeding and the finest educational opportunities should have produced. But the rest . . .

He was simply thankful that the rest were narrow-minded enough to be satisfied with their trust funds, their well-stocked bars and their endless lines of spouses.

It was only fitting that James would have been the one child of Joseph Farmdale to choose an adequate mate. Joseph had foolishly dismissed James's search for a male lover as a passing phase that his eldest son would leave behind. When he hadn't, when it had become obvious that James was determined to remain homosexual, Farmdale had gone into one of the only deep depressions of his life.

It was his son's final accomplishment of a relationship that had brought Joseph out of it. James had written from Vietnam that he had discovered the man he wanted as a life companion. Joseph had been aghast. The existence of the lover had meant some final statement about his son's sexuality that the father had difficulty accepting.

He was sure that his son's lover must be some kind of gold digger. He had ordered extensive investigations of this new person's past. He had discovered, much to his amazement, that James had made a tremendously admirable choice.

The new man was named Alex Kane. "Kane" was an anglicization of a Greek name that an immigration officer at Ellis Island had decided was too unAmerican. "Kane" would do. The family had lived and prospered in one village in Greece for centuries. They had been honorable and proud people, adamantly opposed to the alien Turkish rule that held a stranglehold on their country. That opposition had forced their exile.

They'd come here, to New Hampshire, and settled in Portsmouth where they were fishermen. They had maintained their pride and they had persevered against tremendous odds to establish themselves in the Yankee seaport. This young man, Alex, was the last of their long line. He was the beneficiary of all their heritage.

Brought up by his grandparents after his own father and mother had died in an accident, Alex Kane had been a top student in public schools. He had refused the easy way out of this military service that a college scholarhip offered, instead deciding to enlist in the Marine Corps.

That's where he'd met James. Farmdale remembered his son's glowing letters. There was an enthusiasm in them that could not be denied. That, and an insistence in Alex's rightful place in the family that demanded a response from his father.

Slowly, with the luxury of letters being sent over great distances which allowed Joseph Farmdale to absorb the shock of his son's revelations, Joseph had come to accept his son's position.

He supposed that none of the radicals in the country would have appreciated the precise process he had gone through. Joseph Farmdale simply realized that if his son were, indeed, the repository of all that was decent in the Farmdale tradition — and Joseph did not doubt it to be true — it would have to follow that James could not make a totally foolish decision.

If the scion of the Farmdale line decided that it was good to be homosexual, then it was good to be homosexual. The question was resolved as soon as Joseph Farmdale had defined his correct line of reasoning.

It was his son's murder which had led him on from that starting point. Joseph Farmdale seemed to be studying the green foilage of the New Hampshire mountains now. But the memory of that death was one that he had never truly accommodated himself to. It was painful even now.

If a totally ignorant person could take it upon himself to murder James Farmdale only because he was a homosexual, then the bigotry that was directed towards homosexuals was unacceptable. Utterly, totally and eternally, it had to be wiped out.

That had been Joseph Farmdale's conclusion. It was

James who gave him the vehicle to achieve that goal: His lover, the young man, Alex Kane, who had acted to erase the murderer of his son.

Farmdale had found him in the sleaziest part of San Francisco. He had rescued him. He had given him all that James had requested that he have. Kane had the money that a Farmdale's spouse was entitled to, a great deal of money. He had entry to any office, any home in the country that he desired.

Joseph Farmdale would not have it any other way. Most people assumed that Joseph was incapable of emotions, and indeed he very rarely showed them. Nor did he display passion. His wives would certainly attest to that. But there were things important to Joseph Farmdale, there were things that one simply did not forget. Those things made up a short list. But at the top of the list was his son's memory.

The car pulled to the side of the road. The chauffeur pressed a button to roll down the window that separated the passenger from the driver and the bodyguard who sat in the front seat.

"I think this is the place, Mr. Farmdale," the man said. "As I told you . . ."

"Yes, yes, you told me. I read your report." Joseph Farmdale looked at the narrow dirt road that was immediately in front of them. "Well, drive on. We'll see if they're here."

The huge limousine could only barely make it over the five miles that they had to travel from the highway. But eventually, to the driver's great relief, they came to a large clearing. There was at least an acre of rough lawn here. The brush had all been cut down, and it allowed them a sudden vista of a large lake. Between the entrance to the carefully cared for property and the water was a log cabin. Smoke drifted up its chimney.

There was a Mercedes coupe parked near the house. Farmdale recognized it as the gift he had given Danny Fortelli as a graduation present. "They are here," he announced. Both the driver and the other passenger took revolvers from the shoulder holsters. "Oh, put those away!" Farmdale commanded. "He's not going to harm *me!*"

The two men looked at one another in obvious distress. "Mr. Farmdale, sir ... "

Joseph Farmdale cut off his chauffeur. "I'll have none of that. You're in my employ. He's hardly dangerous to me. Now just wait here."

The driver jumped out of the front door and opened Farmdale's. He still had the revolver in his hand. "Put it away." The driver shrugged and complied. "Wait here," Farmdale repeated.

Using his cane, the necessity for which was a constant annoyance these days, Farmdale walked the rest of the distance to the cabin, carrying only a briefcase.

He didn't knock. He simply opened the door. He wasn't surprised at the sight that was waiting there. Just as he knew he was supposed to be excited by the vistas of the White Mountains, so Joseph Farmdale also knew he should be affected by the image of these two males. They were exercising; Farmdale thought that Alex Kane was always exercising. He and Danny Fortelli were wearing only those silly things that athletes wore — supporters, he remembered the name. He must have had one on himself at some point in his life, perhaps when he'd played polo as a younger man. But he was thankful he didn't recall the indecency of it now.

The supporters were their only covering. The rest of their bodies were exposed. Sweat glistened on their skins. They had obviously been at it for hours again. *Don't they ever tire of all this?* he wondered.

He waited for them to stop; they apparently hadn't noticed him yet, though there was a breeze coming through the doorway. Farmdale decided that Alex was pulling one of his irritating stunts, purposely ignoring him. He would play the same game. He took a chair and continued to watch them.

They were doing those things where you tortured your

stomach. Somehow they had crossed their legs together, for leverage, Farmdale assumed. One would sit up, the other stay on his back. As one descended, the other ascended. Foolishness.

He realized that there were many men and women who would give a fortune to watch this display. Some would be attracted to the youthfulness of Danny's body. Others would appreciate the lines in Kane's torso that were etched so starkly that he appeared to be a medical textbook illustration.

Farmdale, of course, didn't respond to either in any sexual fashion. He simply watched, waiting for them to get over their self-inflicted torture. He had to wait a good fifteen more minutes.

The two men sprawled on their backs on the floor. Their breath was labored, but not nearly so much as it would have been on another man after this kind of workout. Only after their chests had begun to assume a more tolerable cycle of expansion and contraction did they sit up, then stand and face Farmdale.

Danny, the old man was pleased to note, at least had the sense to seem slightly embarrassed by his nearly naked state. He bent down and retrieved a pair of eleastic-waisted shorts to cover himself.

Alex Kane was scowling at Farmdale. "We're retired."

Farmdale lifted a single eyebrow. "You were never employed. How could you be retired?"

Danny seemed surprised. "I thought he worked for you."

Joseph smirked. He had thought that Alex had given that impression. "I don't know that many men who are worth as much as Alex Kane bother with things such as working for a salary."

Alex crossed his arms over his bare chest. "I worked with you."

"If you, in fact, have been in partnership with me for that long a period of time, I would have hoped some sense of graciousness would have been passed on to you, perhaps enough to allow you the taste to offer a visitor a bit of refreshment."

"I'll get it," Danny offered. "What would you like? We don't have much. Herbal teas, some wine . . ."

"Wine would be appreciated."

"I don't want visitors," Kane hadn't relaxed his arms.

Farmdale waited a moment before answering, "For all my years I have had to tolerate unexpected, unappreciated, unwanted, inconvenient, unannounced visits from my relatives. It is a great pleasure to finally be in the other position. I am visiting my family. I expected to be treated with courtesy."

The word "family" hit Alex Kane. He closed his fists in anger. Danny watched, puzzled. His curiosity wasn't assauged when Alex announced, "Give him some wine."

Danny delivered a full glass to Joseph Farmdale in a short time. "Alex," he turned to his lover, "we shouldn't stand around all sweaty like this."

"The odor is not the most enjoyable," Farmdale said as he sipped the wine, gratified to discover that it was one of his favorite St. Emilions. Kane had learned some things.

"We're not worried about the smell, Farmdale," Alex said gruffly. "But it's not healthy to work out and then stand around this way."

"It is certainly not enjoyable for me to have to witness you in such embarrassingly scanty clothing."

"I know," Alex kept his same tone of voice, "it must upset your sense of propriety."

Farmdale sipped more of his wine. "Danny, would you mind bringing the bottle over here. I may need more of this to fortify myself while you two clean off."

• • •

Farmdale had gotten halfway through the wine by the time the pair had come back from the second floor of their house. The sounds of the shower had at least meant that they had running water.

Danny was obviously still reacting to Farmdale's presence. He had put on a quite reasonable set of clothes, a pair of khaki trousers, loafers, a polo shirt. His hair was still damp from the shower. Kane, probably in defiance, had only put on a pair of gym shorts.

No one made any attempt at civil conversation. Farmdale immediately went into the business at hand. "I've some papers for you to sign. Some are simple forms for the maintenance of your trust. I must assume since you've not been in contact with me for the past few weeks that you no longer wish me to handle your affairs."

He opened his briefcase and brought out a folder. "This is a series of documents which transfer responsibility — including a power of attorney — to a bank in Boston. I assume you'll find it a worthy institution for your needs. This," he brought out another set of papers, "is necessary for your estate to be transferred from my own bank in California. You should also, it's always advisable at times such as this, renew your will. It's enclosed. The bank will want to review it with you."

"I don't want to talk to any fucking bank."

"I've told them what a difficult customer they should expect you to be. They're prepared to do all the necessary transactions by mail."

Farmdale poured himself still more wine. "My doctors would have a fit if they knew I was imbibing this much."

Danny and Alex stared at the piled documents as though they contained some kind of time bomb. Farmdale watched the effect of his little scheme and was delighted to see its apparent success.

"Don't you have something else to say to us?" Danny asked.

"Why bother? You are an adult in the eyes of this state, also in Massachusetts. You have the right to make your own decisions. This other one," he waved at Alex Kane, "is so pigheaded that discussion is seldom worthwhile with him. He most certainly is an adult in any event. From the tone of your question I have to assume you've practiced your lines and perfected your defenses. You have the right to your own lives."

Farmdale finished the wine with a loud appreciative smack of his lips. "You've also done me a great favor. When I was in school we often came up to this part of the country. I think it must have been that some of my mates skiied." Farmdale was obviously announcing that he would never have done anything that foolish.

"We had a favorite inn. The Red Crow. It's only a few miles from here. Having flown all the way from California, I've determined to enjoy the place anew. I'll be there for a few days if you'd like to reach me. Perhaps we could have dinner?"

"No." Alex Kane stood up. "We don't want to go to dinner."

Farmdale stood as well. "If you change your mind." He held out a hand. Kane reluctantly came across the room and shook it. Danny followed suit. "You can find the inn in the phone book."

"We don't have a phone."

"I do think you must have a dime for a pay phone, Alex." Then Farmdale smiled and made his way back to the car.

• • •

Alex was still sitting in the same chair he had taken when Farmdale left. Danny finally broke their brooding silence. "What's wrong?"

Alex wouldn't look him in the eye. "I don't dare move. I know he left it here. I know the bastard left it somewhere we'd find it and I can't . . ."

"Left what?"

"The book."

"What book? Alex, you're not talking sense."

"There's always a book, Danny. It always has a red leather binding. He could never just leave a report or have a manila folder. There had to be a book. He had to have it bound. He had to have it all neat and tidy the way the goddamned Farmdales always had everything."

"What's in the book, Alex?"

"Don't you remember? When we were in Boston, when we met? When I told you all I knew about you?" Danny nodded his head yes; he certainly did remember that frightening encounter with the power of information. When Alex was investigating Danny's case he had confronted Danny with his own life story in a matter of a few hours. Now Danny remembered: Alex had read it to him from a book with red leather binding.

"But, what difference does a book make? We can just ignore it."

"Can we? Can we really?" Alex looked at Danny. His lover had known the broad outlines of Alex's work. He had always talked about perhaps joining Alex in his labor once he had finished college. But Alex had always assumed that Danny knew enough, he had gone through enough. There was no need to burden the kid with more. Once you'd been blackmailed, attacked on the streets of your home city and forced into prostitution, you had more than enough experience for a nineteen-year-old.

Danny didn't know the power of those books. The way their computer printouts made sense of random acts, the manner in which they produced patterns where no one else had even seen connections. When one did see that power ...

Danny stood up and walked over to the chair where Farmdale had sat. He didn't see a thing. Then he felt under the cushion. There it was. A red leather book, carefully bound in a fine old Spanish fashion.

"Don't open it, Danny," Alex said.

But Danny had already begun reading the first page.

X

Tim Ranson stood in a bar off Hennepin Avenue. It was early, but he was taking good advantage of happy hour and was well on his way to being drunk.

He looked around at the crowd of men that had gathered, most of them in their office clothes. *Bunch of perverts.* What else could he think after what had happened to Ralph? And after what else had been reported in this morning's newspaper. The *Tribune* had the story on the front page. There was lots of gay news on the front page nowadays in Minneapolis. All of it was bad.

The director of one of the big gay community organizations had left town. That wouldn't have been news. But he'd left town with the entire annual budget of the group. *Rip their own off.* It was to be expected, Tim decided. Not one of them had any respect for the others.

There was another story as well. Another of the gay bars, one of those that proudly announced itself as gay owned — implying that others were part of some mafia conspiracy — had been closed when it was discovered that the fire exits had been purposely blocked. The owner had claimed he had nothing to do with it, but the files of the city safety office showed he'd been warned for the same infraction numerous times before.

What a bunch of scum.

Who just happened to be gay.

Tim thought that one was worth another double Vodka on the rocks. What an efficient drink it was, nearly pure alcohol that could knock you out faster than anything else in the bar.

The bartender filled the glass without comment. He was obviously used to the ones who came in at this time of day and tried to anesthesize themselves with the half-price drinks the boss used to lure them in. They'd get so drunk so quickly that they wouldn't stop when the place reverted to full prices for watered-down drinks in another hour.

Actually, it wasn't going to work too well for Tim. He wasn't used to drinking this much. He'd tried these past few days. He'd taken a leave of absence from Farmdale Industries. There hadn't been any hassle about that. He'd spent the time moving; he couldn't stand the idea of staying in the same apartment, not even in the same building. He'd spent a small fortune from his savings on the necessary deposits for a new one-bedroom place.

He'd refused to keep any of the things he and Ralph had purchased together. That had meant a lot of shopping. He'd gotten new furniture for his small living room today at Dayton's. Thank god for the savings he'd accumulated and the fat check he had been collecting from his job.

He downed half his drink. He should go back to work soon. The schedule would do him good, make some sense out of the hours of the day. He didn't have that now. He'd find himself sleeping in the afternoon and then, at night, reading endless numbers of paperback books to keep his mind occupied.

Actually, there was something here that could do that for him awfully well. A new man had walked into the bar. He looked tough, real tough. He had a bodybuilder's muscles and a kind of bravado about him that appealed to Tim. It was the same kind of surface masculinity that Mike Ahern, his co-pilot, had.

Rough Trade. That's what the guy was. God, Tim hadn't thought of that term in years. But it sure sounded appealing to him now. A straight man who only wanted a blow job, someone who might even throw in a few threatening, demeaning remarks about cocksuckers. *We deserve those.* Tim was getting hard at the thought. Straight man, using a gay man, no emotional entanglements, no fantasies about a life together, that made a lot of sense these days in Minneapolis. Who in his right mind would trust another faggot in this city after what's been going on?

But someone else made a move before Tim even had a chance to cross the bar. The other guy was older and less attractive than Tim, but the score didn't seem to mind. He smiled in a gloating way when the bar patron had introduced himself. They talked and, after only a few words, left their unfinished drinks on the counter and walked out.

I'll get him next time, Tim vowed. *Him or someone like him. No more faggots.*

No one else in the bar appealed to Tim. He didn't really like the tipsy sensations that were coming over him; it was time to leave. He left a tip and walked out. He found his car where he had left it only a block or so away. When he got in he turned on the radio. Any kind of noise was welcome company at this point.

There was some kind of talk program on the air, but Tim wasn't paying much attention to it until some words slipped into his consciousness and he began to listen.

" . . . While we've all been insistent upon the civil rights of all our people, there comes a time when decent people must say stop. That time has come in Minnesota. I have been in the forefront of the battle for gay rights. I have done so believing that gay people should have the same opportunities for fair housing, fair employment and fair treatment before the law.

"But rights bring with them responsibilities. It's become clear that the gay community of the Twin Cities has not been willing to bear those responsibilities. Until they do, we, the family people of our state, must protect our children and our selves from their capricious, unfeeling behavior . . ."

The guy was right. Tim Ranson wasn't going to argue with him, that much was for sure. The voice droned on.

" . . . It's time for all of us to re-examine the priorities with which we live. Yes, the First Amendment has played an important part in our civil liberties. But now feminists are showing that the protection of free speech is something that hurts. Yes, we thought that gay rights were the correct thing and we tried to do right by advocating them. But giving gay people free rein has only provided their most predatory members with the license to kill, corrupt and misuse one another. For their own protection, we have to look at just what it is that we have loosened on society.

"These are painful things for a man with my reputation to have to acknowledge. But there is no doubt about the dangers that are threatening our families and our moral values.

"Every thinking mother and father, brother and sister, knows that it's true. The endless stories that have been reported in the press have proven it. We can't deny that gay rights have backfired."

I sure as hell can't, Tim agreed.

"That's been this week's program from State Representative Andrew Marston. Mr. Marston's position tonight has represented a drastic change in his political agenda. He invites you to respond to his observations. For a transcript of this speech, simply write this station. Mr. Marston thinks that this topic is so important, you needn't enclose the usual fee for that transcript. Just send your name and address on a post card."

XI

Now Joseph Farmdale remembered the attraction of the Red Crow Inn. The breakfast was remarkable. Really homemade bread, homemade sausages as well. The coffee was strong and fresh. The jams were probably made right here in this kitchen. He was delighted with the meal. He was also delighted when he saw Alex Kane and Danny Fortelli walk into the dining room. There was no doubt that his strategy had worked.

The sadness wasn't there. Farmdale saw it immediately. Instead there was anger, great anger. Alex's eyes glistened with it. It was always remarkable to see how the green in his eyes shone when this particular emotion had taken over Alex's person. There was an iridescence about him. He was like some kind of beacon.

The two men took their seats without a word. Farmdale waved toward the proprietor of the inn who smiled and brought coffee to the table. "We've eaten," Alex said to her when she offered menus.

Only when she'd left them alone did Kane speak again. "You're a bastard."

"There's a plane at Logan waiting for you. At the usual terminal. On it you'll find further briefing papers. There's more data than you'd normally expect. The case is more complicated and more dangerous."

Kane didn't respond. Farmdale looked over to Danny. "Are you sure you're ready to begin this now? I know that Alex has . . . sheltered you in the past."

Danny smiled vaguely. "Have I really been sheltered?" It seemed a personal joke to him. "Have I really?" No one spoke for a moment. Danny continued, "I guess I *better* be ready, Mr. Farmdale. Like you said, I'm an adult now. Mommy and daddy can't protect me any longer." Danny's smile disappeared. "Yes, I'm ready."

"There's money on the plane as well. I trust you have more than enough in any event. But . . . "

"Fine," Alex stopped Farmdale's speech. "I burnt all the papers you brought. Nothing's changed."

Farmdale nodded. He had expected nothing else.

The two men stood. "You're a bastard," Alex Kane repeated.

Farmdale met his glare. "One should learn not to blame the messenger for tragedy. That's all I am, Alex, a messenger. You don't have to read my messages and you don't have to trust my dispatches. You don't have to believe my facts, nor do you have to act on them. You choose to do that. You choose to do that . . . for Danny."

Alex closed his eyes. He'd heard the speech or one like it many times before. But the ending had changed. It had always used to be, " . . . for James." Now it was " . . . for Danny." But it was still Joseph Farmdale and it was still Alex Kane.

XII

The campaign advisors were meeting again. This time Andrew Marston wasn't complaining. Not at all. "It's a fucking dream come true."

He waved at the huge pile of mail that filled the center of the conference table. "It's all from a single radio broadcast. The media's eating it up. I have all three networks and Cable Network News all lined up for interviews tomorrow. The New York *Times* is coming to cover the moral revolution in Minnesota. The Washington *Post* is sending a top reporter to interview me."

"Watch out for all them," Luther Angstrom warned. The big Swede was glowering. "Those pinkos aren't going to give up their crusades that easy."

"You're wrong, Luther, wrong. I tell you, we've pulled it off. We have more crime in the gay community here than in any other segment of the population. It's working wonders! The plan to have lots of it directed at other gays is doing the trick perfectly. Not one of them's talking against me."

"That crazy one is," Luther insisted. "The one that runs that center."

"Oh . . ." Andrew dismissed the objection. "He's pissing in the wind. No one's paying attention to him. Not even the real lefties. You know, I don't think they ever really did like the gays, the way they're back peddling on this issue."

"How can you blame them?" Marty O'Brien asked with a grin. "We got child molesters, murderers, sex fiends gone mad, bar owners caught for breaking every rule in the books, everything we could ever have dreamed of."

"Hasn't been a bad scam," Sonny LeBec agreed. He'd had a good time getting at all his competition. Only his own bars had escaped any notice in the press recently. And there was much more to come. He'd seen to it.

"You're set for the next act?" Andrew asked.

LeBec smiled. "It's begun. Real easy. Real expensive, but real easy." He hesitated, waiting either for an acknowledgement of his accomplishment or else an offer to help pay the price. But they all knew how much more he was taking in these days and no one felt a need to underwrite his success. He shrugged. "It'll start in the papers tomorrow, I bet. What about your plans?"

Sonny had turned to Martin Martello. "Oh, on schedule. It's going to really cost me too." Again no one responded. "But I got some set-ups you won't believe. You don't have to worry about that Anderson kid." Martin was referring to Mike Anderson, the gay activist that Luther Angstrom had been concerned with. "He'll get his."

"All of them," Andrew Marston smiled, "they're all going to get theirs. I'm taking another turn to the right tonight. It'll be in the papers tomorrow. This little bit of magic we're pulling has given us the perfect opportunity to justify the change in my positions. I'm going to out-family the Republicans on this one and no one's going to question my motives in the least. Hell, they're all going to be cheering by the time I'm done. Cheering."

The way they will when I get elected to the governor's mansion. Marston didn't have to verbalize that. They all knew he was thinking it; they all were thinking the same thing and liking the sound of it very, very much.

XIII

"I tell you, he couldn't have done it. Dr. Chisle never would have done anything like that." Mike Anderson was pleading with his compatriot, Charlie Tile. Usually Mike was clear, concise and spoke with an air of authority. But the recent events in Minnesota had eroded that strength.

Charlie didn't dislike Mike, but he'd been secretly bristling at all the attention the leader of the community center had been getting. It was too good a shot to pass up, getting at Mike when he was this vulnerable and when he was backing such a stupid cause.

"You've got to be kidding, Anderson. Look, just because you've tumbled with *Dr.* Chisle doesn't mean he's a saint. Your politically correct behavior isn't a communicable disease, you know. He's a typical closeted middle-class queer who only thinks of sex. The way he got into your pants was to talk the right line, that's all. You fell for it.

"The guy's a sex fiend. Hiring kids from poor countries and then using coercion to get them to do what he wants. Get over it, Anderson. He's a lost cause."

"Look, I went and talked to him at the jail. He promised me he's been framed . . ."

"Mike, stop it! Can't you see you're letting your emotions get in the way of your best judgment? He's a classist, ageist, sexist pig and he's getting what he's got coming. You should be happy to have him out of the way."

"He's not." Anderson's voice sounded feeble now. It was hard for him to react to the litany of anti-gay liberation charges when they were directed at a man he was in love with.

"Mike, you're only twenty-five years old. What's a man of nearly forty doing going after you?" There was a distinct and vicious edge to Charlie's voice.

"He's . . . Charlie, he's not like that. I swear. Look, you know damn well he's given the center money, a lot of money. He's closeted to some extent, sure, but he's not like the rest. He at least makes sure that we all have something to work with. He's had fund raisers for our causes in his home, and as for me, well, sure he's older. But he's never used that in any oppressive way."

"He didn't have to," Charlie Tile was studying his fingernails in a faint imitation of a fading movie star. "You never made him work for his little piece."

Mike stood up and made a move toward Charlie. But stopped himself. Violence, he had long ago decided, would never be a part of his life.

"Face it, Mike, he pays for the dinners, he chooses the restaurants, he pays for the airplane tickets for your little vacations, and you put out. He's using you, buying you the same way he bought those starving kids. You just don't want to see how he's oppressing you."

Mike sat back down again. The words sounded right, but somehow the logic didn't. He'd been living on a subsistence income for years while he worked in gay activism. Somehow the chances to have a big meal out and a week in the Florida sun with Allen Chisle just hadn't seemed all that horrible when the dentist had offered them to him.

"He's eroding your politics." With that damning statement, Charlie stood up. "Besides, this is hardly the time for any of us to be backing one of them. For Christ's sake, we have gay murders going on, there are a hundred and one things wrong in this city. We don't have the time or the luxury of appearing to be on the side of one of the guys that have been grabbing the headlines. They've been ruining the reputation of all of us. All of our work is going down the tube.

"You can bring it up to the steering committee if you want to, Mike. But they're going to be on my side on this one for a change. There's no way in hell we're going to go and defend someone like Allen Chisle with the way things are happening in Minneapolis now."

Charlie had stood up and walked out the room. Mike sat stunned in the chair behind his desk. There were the sounds of people chattering in the other offices in the building. He was torn, desperately torn. Right here were the fruits of his years of labors. There was a housing group, an organization that coordinated a whole series of support groups for gay fathers, lesbian mothers, gay and lesbian alcoholics . . . the list went on. It had taken long hard work to get the funding for it all. Mike knew perfectly well that the coalition of church and fraternal organizations and foundations that he had put together was already starting to fall apart. A conservative Lutheran committee was the first to withdraw, citing conflicting priorities, but Mike knew that the wave of gay scandals throughout Minneapolis and its twin city, St. Paul, were the real reason.

All that got mixed up with his even more personal feelings about Allen Chisle's possible connections. He'd been dating Allen for over three years. All Allen's requests for a commitment had been fended off by Mike. He had been the one to insist on an "open relationship" — even though he actually hadn't had sex with anyone else in over a year. It had been a matter of principle to Mike, or so he had thought. Where his principles actually were was becoming less clear to him.

As the head of the center, he had to defend the community against these incredible attacks. As the man who loved Allen Chisle, he couldn't abandon the dentist for political expediency. If Allen needed him during this crisis — and it was obvious he did — then Mike wanted to stand by him.

But what if Allen were part of the reason for the crisis? That part hurt. Not just because it meant that Mike had misjudged Allen politically; it meant that his vision of their relationship with one another had been false, that Mike had been had. It wasn't a good thought.

"Are you Mike Anderson?" Mike looked up when he heard his name spoken. Two men stood in his doorway. One of them appeared to be younger than himself, but not much. He was about 5'10" and had a beautiful face and that loose shirt he was wearing wasn't covering up the build he had underneath. The other was older, maybe thirty. He was cleanshaven. He was wearing only a strapped t-shirt and a pair of jeans. There was smooth skin showing, very smooth skin, the type that usually meant a guy hardly had any body hair. But he certainly had strange green eyes. They were slightly hypnotic, it seemed.

He also had a body, an incredible body with etched muscles apparent on his arms. Everything said that the rest of his torso would be the same.

"Yeah, I'm Mike." He stood up and offered a hand to each of the two visitors, then waved toward empty chairs that sat facing his desk.

He sat down as they did, then realized they hadn't introduced themselves. Before he could ask their names, the older guy had opened up an obviously expensive book, one with deep red binding. He had begun to read.

"You've been seeing a Dr. Allen Chisle for quite some time. Pretty friendly it seems. Dr. Chisle's taken you to Key West a couple of times, to Provincetown one . . ."

"Hold it right there," Mike said sharply. "You guys must

be cops if you have that kind of data. Well, if you think you're going to get me involved in Dr. Chisle's trial . . ."

"You already are involved." The younger man spoke now. "You're in love with him."

"How do you know that?" Mike was stunned by the stark statement.

"It's all over that book. All over your life. I can tell. I know what love looks like."

Mike spat back a response, "Oh, you do?" The guy nodded yes. Mike looked at the handsome youth and suddenly, for some reason he'd never understand, he said, "You do." Then he looked over at the other man. He took a deep breath. "Look, let's get out of here. The phone's going to start ringing, there'll be lots of interruptions. I'm hungry anyway. There's a restaurant down the street."

"You're on," Alex Kane replied.

• • •

"It just doesn't make sense." Mike had listened while Alex Kane had finished reading the dossier on Allen Chisle. There hadn't been anything new in the report. Oh, a couple tricks Allen had had, but they'd been with men close to his own age. It was Mike's own fault if there was any "infidelity" — he'd been the one, he had reminded himself, who'd wanted that open relationship.

"I've seen the evidence the police have. It looks open and shut. There are signed agreements, there's the testimony of the kids, including the one he had in his apartment. He didn't do anything outlandish with them on the surface of it, but there was the definite element of coercion. He made them give him blow jobs and let him fuck them."

Danny studied Mike for a second. "Does that make sense to you?"

"What do you mean?"

"That he'd want to fuck them. Was that what you and he . . ."

"Well ...," Mike blushed a bit, "No it doesn't make sense. Sure, we would switch around, but, well, I ... he'd rather I was doing that. No big deal, I mean it's not a part of my macho self or something, it's just that ..."

Danny put up a hand. "Look, I understand." He smirked at Alex. "I understand perfectly. People have preferences. But if Dr. Chisle's preference was to have you do it, why would he all of a sudden be going to these lengths to start doing the fucking himself?"

"It's typical." Mike gathered all the political analyses of sex he had ever read. "I'm a big blond Swede. He wanted to get fucked by me. These kids were dark skin, short, he wanted to fuck them. It's all political, racist shit." He was wringing his hands as he talked.

"Does that sound like Allen Chisle to you?" Alex asked.

"No. But, damn it, we've all internalized so much of that crap. Of course it could be true of him. So he acted one way with me, then he turned around and acted another way with these guys. What happened between us doesn't matter."

"What does matter," Alex said in a slow voice, "Is what you thought of him. It matters whether or not you think he was capable of this kind of thing. You've been seeing him for a long time. You're bright, observant and sensitive. What do you think? Did Allen Chisle do what he's charged with?"

"No." That was a definite statement. "He just *couldn't* have."

"Then that's what we'll go on," Alex replied. "That he couldn't have done it. Then we have to find out who set him up and why they did it. What about that question? Do you have any clues?"

"Not a one," Mike answered. "I wish I did, but I can't think of a single damned reason why anyone who knew Allen would put him in this position."

"Listen, Mike. We need your help. There are too many things going on here. There are too many mysteries. I'm betting there's just a single answer to all of them. But it's going to take work to figure it out. Will you work with us?"

Any conflicts between the center's needs and those of Allen, between politics and helping the man he had been seeing for so long, had disappeared. *Then that's what we'll go on . . . he couldn't have done it.* Those words produced a clarity to Mike's thoughts for the first time since this whole mess began. "Of course I'll help."

XIV

When Danny woke up in their hotel room the next morning, Alex was already standing up, looking out the window. They were in one of the buildings in the IDS Center that was built around a huge glass-covered courtyard. The big king-sized bed was luxurious, but the room was so large that it wasn't too big for the scale of the space.

Danny got out of bed, stretched and then went to stand by Alex. Both men were naked. Danny snaked an arm around Alex's waist and followed his partner's gaze down to the floor of the courtyard. There were fast-moving crowds there, all of them rushing to work, to appointments, to the big department stores that were nearby.

"Why do they have this enclosed?" Danny asked.

"The weather. Minneapolis is too frigid in the winter for a lot of people to tolerate. In the summer it's nearly as bad. The temperature and the humidity go way, way up. So they have spaces like this. Over there," Alex pointed through the glass courtyard to the street where they could see corridors built over the streets, "they have a whole series of passages they call skyways connecting all the buildings. They're for the same thing — protecting people from the weather."

"Is that what you're thinking about?" Danny asked.

"The weather? No. I'm just thinking about all those

people. I'm wondering how many of them are gay, how many of them are going to be caught up in all this shit that's going on. I need to do that, Danny, when I'm out here. When I'm going to have to face down an enemy as violent and horrible as this one, I have to remember why I'm doing it, and who I'm doing it for.

"Look at them. They're just going about their business. Innocent people. A lot of them are gay. All they want is a decent job, a house or an apartment, a lover or at least some decent boyfriends. They want a little pleasure and they want some good times. That's all most people in this world want.

"Instead they're getting . . . " Alex's voice trailed off. He knew he didn't have to finish his sentences.

Danny squeezed a little then let go of his lover. He saw that Alex had already had coffee delivered. He went over and poured himself a cup. There was a paper on the table by the service. Alex had already opened it.

Danny sat down and drank his coffee while he read the front page. He put the paper down after a few minutes. "This is why you're looking out there now, isn't it?"

Alex nodded slightly.

Danny went back to the paper and finished the lead article. The headline said it all: Gay Murderer Lurks Hennepin Avenue Bars.

"Let's shower and get dressed, Alex. We're going to have to go find Mike Anderson. This is getting even worse."

• • •

A television station mobile unit was parked outside the apartment building that Mike had given them as his address. Alex and Danny moved through the crowds and up the stairs to the third floor. Mike was at the door talking to a reporter in an agitated voice.

"No, you can't come in. No, I have no comment. I don't know any more about the murders than you do. I don't want to appear on television to defend the gay community against the charges. There are no charges yet. What's with you people? A month ago you wouldn't have bought this line. You wouldn't be acting like a bunch of rednecks sniffing out some gay corruption. A month ago . . ."

"Things were a lot different a month ago," Muriel Stang said. Danny recognized her face from a television broadcast last night.

"Well, this hasn't changed. I have no comment. You cannot come in and set up your cameras. There is no interview."

"We'll remember that, Mike," Muriel said with an acid smile. "We'll remember that the next time you want us to edit the coverage on a gay pride parade."

"We never asked you to edit your coverage. We just wanted you to show something besides the fringes, something other than the cross-dressers and the . . . "

"Don't bother, Mike," the journalist said, "the way things are going, you won't be having a gay pride parade this year."

The imperious broadcaster turned on her heel and marched down the stairs with her obedient camera crew in tow. No one bothered to pay any attention to Alex and Danny as they passed the pair of men in the hallway.

Mike Anderson slumped his big body against the door frame. He was dressed in a pair of jeans and a pullover shirt. Alex noted what a large man he was, more of a football player than political activist. He was healthy looking; a slight layer of spongy flesh didn't hide a well-developed physique. This was not a guy that a man interested in boys would go after.

"You might as well come on in." Mike turned and Danny and Alex followed him into his small apartment. Mike closed the door. The phone began ringing immediately. Mike went over, picked it up, immediately depressed the switch to cut the connection and then left the receiver off the hook. "It's been going like crazy.

"I remember when we used to beg them to give us coverage of anything. I used to plead for them to interview anyone in the community who could give a positive image or an intelligent answer to their questions. It was like pulling teeth. But now they want daily quotes and running commentary."

Alex was looking around the small studio apartment. The wall were covered with posters announcing political rallies and denouncing every "ism" in the book. There were cases full of the expected volumes on gay liberation. The bed was a simple mattress on the floor. The gallery kitchen was piled with soiled dishes and pans. There wasn't much on the open shelves in the way of food; Mike obviously lived, ate and breathed his political convictions. Alex knew that no one could be interested in him who didn't have some kind of interest in the same issues. Dr. Allen Chisle was looking more and more like an interesting person to Kane.

"You've seen the papers?" Mike asked.

Danny answered, "Yes, that's why we're here. What's going on?"

Mike sat down on the mattress. There were only two wooden-back chairs at a tiny table for his visitors to sit on. They took their seats and waited for a response.

"I just don't know. After the immigration scandals and the bars getting busted for breaking all the health and safety codes ... " His voice trailed off. "How can you fight that? How can you fight it when the city closes businesses that are obviously endangering the community's well being? Or when men are supposedly kidnapping and blackmailing innocent children ... "

"How do you fight murderers?" Alex asked.

Mike just shook his head. "Look, there have been three reported in the last two nights. They are clearly killings of gay men by gay men. All three victims were seen cruising in bars. They all were seen picking someone up. We have to assume it was their tricks. It was our own attacking our own."

"Was it?" Alex's question had a sharp tone to it. He'd seen

this kind of thing before.

"What's going to happen now?" Danny picked up his own line of questioning.

"The police are combing the city. They're talking to — and scaring the shit out of — everyone who knew the three men. They're going to send undercover agents into the bars. They're taking photographs of patrons on the sly, beginning tonight. They've announced all this over the media. It's produced something just short of total panic around town. There are just too many people who are terrified of being identified as bar patrons. That, and a whole lot of people are terrified of the danger that the bars seem to represent these days."

Mike went to his refrigerator, took out a bottle of orange juice and poured himself a glass. He offered his visitors some, but they declined. "Then there's Representative Marston."

"I read about him in the paper," Alex said. "Who is he? What's he doing in all this?"

"He used to be the very best friend of every good cause in the city. Our man at the state capitol." Mike said the sentence with a sarcastic voice. "I never trusted the guy. He had the right viewpoints, but none of them were ever put into action. I mean, he was all for women's rights, but no matter how often he talked about the ERA he always treated women like second-class citizens, second-class citizens he wanted to get into bed. He'd say he was for gay rights, but he was always uncomfortable around me, that's for sure. It seemed more acceptable if a gay guy was in drag, somehow that made more sense to him. But anyone my size and my appearance made him feel funny.

"I don't know, I can't prove it, but that's my impression of the guy.

"In any event, he's made this big turn-around. Now he's appealing to people in the political center to come out against gays. He's been saying that the experiment in gay rights — that's his term: "experiment" — has failed. He wants people to rally around him in a new, supposedly still liberal, political coalition that would be economically aligned with the Democratic Party, but morally somewhere to the right of Genghis Khan."

"Is he succeeding?" Danny asked.

"Oh, sure he is. And you know where a lot of his success is coming from? Gay men. They're terrified of getting caught up in this net, either as victims of some strange and unknown criminal figures after them — you can't blame people for that — or else they're frightened that their good reputations are going to get smeared by the campaign."

Alex Kane showed no emotion on his face. There was just a calmness about him. It was neither sadness, nor was it resignation. Danny looked at him, he especially studied Alex's eyes. He could see the glint there, that brightness that came with Alex's fury.

XV

Larry Lawson stood in the gay bar and studied the crowd. What an easy score this was going to be. He had a nice wad of bills in his pocket, a down payment from Sonny LeBec. Sonny was one hell of a guy to have given Larry such a cushy job. He provided too — sure as hell, Sonny LeBec provided. Larry had his return ticket to Vegas already in hand.

Larry usually only got hired for the tough jobs, the real tough jobs that come from the Nevada underworld. He was so used to the danger and risk involved in going after other hoods that the idea of just making it rough for a gay guy was a piece of cake.

Sonny had been very specific and very easy about his job order. Larry had to pick up some fruit in a bar. He had to take care of him. Sometime in the far distant past murder was something that must have bothered Larry. But now? Now it was something that came with the territory.

He looked around for a mark. That was another thing. Sonny wanted it done clean and easy. It had to be a guy who obviously belonged in the bar, one who knew what was going on. Sonny expected there'd be undercover cops out this time. They could be trouble. That's why the big guns like Larry had been brought in for the second round. Larry could smell a cop a mile away.

Like that one guy who was just wearing a tank top across the bar from Larry and trying to give him the eye. He was too old for Larry's taste. Not that Larry really got into guys, you have to understand that. But if it was part of the job to pork a young butt, well, that could be done — if it was part of the job and Larry *had* to do it.

But not one as old as that. The guy didn't look bad — nice muscles, firm flesh. *He probably has a nice ass,* Larry thought. But the idea was a fleeting one. It just wouldn't be right to prong someone nearly your own age. Besides, something told Larry that man could be a cop. Just a suspicion, but it was enough.

Larry smiled as he thought how appropriate he was for the job. He figured a good-looking guy like himself with a big dork would go over real well in a gay bar. These flits sure should be turned on to him. He put his back to the bar and stretched out his arms, still holding his beer in one hand. His polyester pants must be showing off his crotch to good effect. There was one young guy over across the room who was giving him the eye.

This one was more like it.

He was so handsome that Larry could even imagine him as a girl. His lips were a deep red, his skin was smooth and his hair was dark and curly. Too bad the kid seemed to have too much chest hair. That wasn't so hot. Larry would have liked to combine this one's appearance with the hairlessness of the first man who'd been looking at him. But Sonny said to get it over with fast, so Larry would compromise.

He walked the few steps to the young man's perch on a ledge against the wall. "How ya doin'?" Larry asked.

"Just fine." The kid had a good voice. Nice and smooth. Larry reached out and put a hand on one of his thighs. Whew, those were nice legs, good strong legs. This kid could probably throw a mean fuck. Larry was getting hard thinking about that. Thinking about the way someone with this kind of build could just milk his cock.

They went through the motions. Larry hadn't ever had a hard time when he'd had to pick up a gay guy. Just the same kind of mindless chatter that you had to give a broad in a singles joint would do. All they ever had to have was enough encouragement to believe you were dealing with them as a *person*. Oh, how they hated to be treated like meat.

Well, kid, let's make believe you're a person, just enough to let me taste the slabs of meat you got around my cock.

It was easy as pie. Just easy. Larry was walking out of the bar in a couple minutes, this kid following him with all the willingness he'd expected. Sonny wanted it done quick? Larry delivered. He'd done it in less than ten minutes. He'd just walked into the bar and pulled out the best looking thing with no effort at all.

The kid had agreed to walk back to Sonny's hotel, a fleabag a few blocks down Hennepin in one of the few areas of the downtown that hadn't been rebuilt yet. No nosy room clerk at this time of night. Nothing to interfere with what Larry had to do. He checked his watch. It was so early he could still catch the red-eye back to Vegas tonight.

What a fucking easy score.

Once they were in the room, Larry turned the lock on the door. He turned around and stared at the kid. "What's your name?"

"Danny." Kid had a nice smile.

"Well, Danny, I'm going to show you a real good time. You take care of old Larry, and Larry'll take care of you." *And then I'll kill you.* "Let's see what you got kid."

The smile didn't leave the young guy's face. Larry had to admit this was one time he wouldn't mind giving a gay guy a tumble. Hell, a hole's a hole. He wasn't about to say that to the guys back in Vegas, but hell, look at that body.

"I think we have some talking to do first."

Larry's smile disappeared. "No we don't, kid. We got better things to do than talk." Larry hated talking with people when he was going to do them.

"I want to talk, Larry."

"Then why you smiling like that?" Was the kid trying to egg him on purposely?

"I always smile when I meet strangers from out of town."

"What makes you think I am? You don't know I'm not from here."

"Oh, but you're not. I asked a couple friends. They'd never seen you before. Where are you from, Larry?"

"Kid, I don't have time for a lot of conversation. Come on, now. You got me all hot and bothered. Let's get it on."

"I told you, Larry, we have to talk first."

The kid was crazy. Larry might have put up with this shit to get him out of a bar, but it wasn't going to be worth doing it if it meant all this work. Too bad, it would have been a great lay. Larry knew it.

"Now, Danny, don't be difficult." Larry moved across to his suitcase. He hadn't carried his gun on the streets. It was too bulky, especially with the silencer on its barrel. It was amazing how quiet an automatic pistol could be with a silencer. "Let me just get some poppers." Larry went into the bag that was sitting on the bureau and reach for his gun.

He heard Danny's movement before he could see it. It was just a very quick couple of steps barely audible on the carpeted floor. Then there was a *whoosh*, followed by an incredible pain in his arm. The fucking asshole was standing on his suitcase. The metal edges were digging into Larry's wrist.

"I don't like poppers, Larry." The kid was smiling.

Larry let out a scream. As soon as he did the door burst open with a loud crash. Larry was trapped, he couldn't move with the young guy standing on his arm that way. But the noise was so sudden and unexpected that he had to look to see what was going on.

It was the other guy from the bar. The strange looking

one. He looked angry rather than surprised. "What the hell happened? How the hell did you get there?" The newcomer was screaming at Danny, not Larry.

"I'm a gymnast, remember? A simple double flip off the mattress." Then, as though to emphasize his point, Danny did a quick little jump. A jump so fast that Larry's hand couldn't escape from the grip of the his suitcase's edge. There was a loud snap as his arm broke. Then Larry passed out from the pain.

XVI

They were back in their room at their own hotel. It was late now. There was hardly any traffic down on the courtyard of the IDS Center. Danny was on the bed, his arms behind his head, as he seemed to be studying the ceiling. Alex sat in a chair, still dressed, staring into space.

"Is this the big break?" Danny asked.

"Maybe. Probably not. This guy, LeBec, is a big gay bar owner, that's what Mike Anderson said. He's shady, but he's not the really big time. Besides, a gay bar owner isn't the kind to scare his customers out of the bars. He certainly shouldn't be hiring paid guns to get rid of his customers."

"So you believe what he said?"

"People in that much pain usually don't have the ability to lie well, Danny. He was in a *lot* of pain."

"I didn't know if he was right-handed or left-handed." Danny's reply was very matter of fact.

"So you made sure neither one would ever work again." Alex didn't seem to be questioning Danny's decision.

"At least not on a gun trigger."

They were silent. The courtyard had an eeriness about it at this time of night. They only had a small lamp turned on in the room. It was dusk-like.

"Alex, is this what it always feels like?"

"How do you mean that?" Alex's voice seemed to carry great hurt with it. It was as though he knew what the question really meant, but he was hoping he was wrong.

"When you fight someone like that, someone who would have killed a weaker person, one who didn't have my skills and couldn't have jumped like that. Is this what it always feels like?"

"I was outside. I would have saved you."

"If you could have, I know you would have. But there was a silencer. I could have believed him when he said he was just after poppers."

"But you didn't. I trusted you not to."

Danny thought longer. "You're not answering my real question, Alex."

"You tell me what you feel like, then I'll answer."

"Like I was making believe I was Sy. I was making believe that Sy had fought back, that he had the ability to fight back and save himself. Like I was going to bring him back if I succeeded. I did succeed. But Sy didn't come back."

Alex was silent.

"Do I have to feel this every time?"

"Yes."

Danny rolled over on the mattress and buried his head in his elbow. Alex came over to his lover and covered Danny's body with his own as though he thought he could offer some protection by doing it.

"We don't have to do this, Danny. We can go back to New Hampshire. We can stay on the lake this time. We don't have to . . ."

"Yes we do." Alex was startled when Danny talked. He'd expected tears. There weren't any. "We have to do it so there aren't any more Sy's. We have to do it because we know how. You know how and you're going to teach me how. We have to do it because there could be a lot more pigs like that if we don't. And they could create a lot more Sy's. We had to do it."

Alex reached around Danny's body and held his lover tightly.

XVII

Mike Anderson was knocking at their door the next morning. He was a little startled when Alex opened the door wearing only a pair of gym shorts. Behind him Danny was dressed the same way. There was the distinct odor of a locker room, as though the pair had been exercising for hours.

"Come on in. We're finished, I guess. We're going to have to shower. Why don't you call room service while we're doing it? Get us all some breakfast." Alex told the young activist what they would have and encouraged him to order anything he wanted.

It seemed to take the pair a long time to clean up, so long that Mike couldn't help wondering if they were . . . Sure they were. He smiled. They didn't come out of the bathroom until after the meal had been delivered and set up by a bellhop.

Danny and Alex were fully dressed when they came to the table. Mike couldn't help but be a little disappointed. He supposed it wasn't right to want to keep on looking at their bodies when there was business to do, but . . . well, he wouldn't have minded the distraction for a while.

He put down the paper as they took their seats. "We have a day's reprieve. Nothing here today."

He caught them exchanging a conspiratorial look. Danny reached over and leafed through the newspaper. "Nothing," he agreed. Mike was a little angry that he hadn't been believed. He just didn't realized that Danny wasn't looking for the same story.

The phone rang before he could make any comment. Just as well. He supposed these guys had to double-check everything.

Alex had stood up and answered the call. He spoke in sharp monotones to someone he evidently didn't like. Only occasionally would there be a complete sentence. "Just tell me, will you!" Mike looked at Danny with a worried expression after a couple of outbursts like that.

Danny was putting jam on his English muffin. "It's his family." That seemed to amuse the young man a lot.

Alex slammed the phone down and stalked over to rejoin them. "Chisle is out this morning. We have to finish up and go meet him."

"He couldn't be!" Mike insisted. "I mean, they refused him bail. One of the charges was kidnapping. It's a federal crime, a capital offense. There was no bail."

Danny looked over to the clock on their bedstand. "It's nearly ten in the morning, our time. Alex's just pissed off it took so long to arrange."

"You're sure?" Mike was incredulous.

"He's sure," Danny assured him.

• • •

An hour later they were back in the hotel room. This time Allen Chisle was with them. The dentist had passionately embraced his friend Mike as soon as the door had closed.

"You didn't have to wait that long, I was ready on the street."

"So was I," Allen insisted. "I was waiting to get inside for your sake."

"*My* sake? Allen, I'm the one who goes on television."

"Well, I do too now. So I guess that's one less problem we'll have to deal with."

Their arms clutched one another all over again.

Danny seemed to enjoy the sight. Alex Kane wasn't joining in on the festivities though; he was already pacing the floor in frustration.

Finally, Allen and Mike seemed to regain some control over themselves. "Who are you? How did you arrange that?"

Alex was curt. "It wasn't that big a problem. A few phone calls, that's all. Look, we've got to talk."

Allen looked to Mike with a silent question. "Just trust them. It doesn't look as though we have any choice."

The four were all finally seated. Alex continued. "I need to know everything about these kids and you. Don't leave out a single fact. The truth, all of it."

"I didn't do it. I mean, not like they said I did." Allen Chisle was a big man. His stomach was a little pudgy, and his hair was receding. But there was something so intrinsically good-natured about him that Alex and Danny could understand what had attracted Mike.

"I believe you. Forget their accusations. I don't need to hear your defense against those charges. But you have to understand, someone was able to make a case against you that looks awfully good. Now, there's got to be something in the story that contains at least a grain of that case. There's enough there to construct the fabrications around it in a way that makes sense when the story's retold."

"Yes, yes, of course there is. I mean, I did hire the boy who testified against me. He was from Haiti. At least that's what they told me . . ."

"*They!* Who's that?"

"People I know. One of my patients is heavily involved in finding homes for orphans from abroad. They sponsor their entrance into the United States and then have to find them work. Paco was supposed to be eighteen. That's what he said. They told me he was gay. I wasn't interested in him sexually, but I knew he had to . . . Look, you remember when

83

they brought in all the gay guys from Cuba, in that boat flotilla? Well, I was even deeper in my closet then. I've always felt a little guilty that I hadn't helped those guys out.

"They're our kind, I figured, but I was so scared I didn't dare come forward. Sure, I sent an anonymous donation, but that was all. I learned later that lots of them had to spend extra time in the camps the government set up because there weren't homes for them. If I hadn't been so frightened of myself and my reputation, at least one of them could have been leading a different kind of life."

"Why didn't you tell me about this?" Mike insisted.

"Because I thought you'd think I was just doing it to be politically correct for your sake. I wasn't. I was doing it for *me*. I was just making up for a past mistake, a time I hadn't acted. I figured I'd get Manuel set up and then I'd introduce you. They told me the kid would have to back to Guatemala if I didn't take him. They'd found out his sexuality and he wasn't going to find another placement."

"I still want to know who *they* are," Alex Kane wasn't giving up the question.

"Oh, Mrs. Martello. Her husband, Martin Martello, is some kind of big exporter/importer. I've been taking care of their teeth for years. I trusted her."

"Do you know this woman?" Alex asked Mike.

"I've never heard of her before, or her husband."

"We have another name to check out," Alex said to Danny. "Martin Martello."

XVIII

"Everything's on schedule." Andrew Marston was gloating as he presided over his advisory council once more. "It's just perfect."

"Not perfect," Sonny LeBec contradicted him. "My hit last night didn't work out. I haven't heard from him."

Marston refused to be concerned. "So one of your guns ran out on you with your money. One little detail isn't going to derail this operation now."

"You don't understand, it was Larry the Gun from Vegas. I'm talking about one of the most professional enforcers in the business."

"Larry?" Luther Angstrom recognized the name. "It sure isn't like Larry to mess an assignment."

"But he did this time. Big deal. You guys don't exactly deal with the most responsible element of society." Marston was being lordly over his advisors these days. It was as though he could sniff his victory and their eventual replacement. It was a mistake. Every man at the table was able to sense what he was thinking. A letter opener appeared in Angstrom's hand and he began to pick at his nails, an unmistakable sign.

Marston ignored him. The press had been perfect. No one — at least hardly anyone — dared to question his new moral revolution. He had had one disappointment: The feminists who were sponsoring the anti-pornography laws had come over to his side. It seemed they were the most willing members of the Minnesota political establishment when it came to believing the worst about gay men. That meant Marston was saddled with them again. He'd hoped he could dump the women's movement when the moral crusade began. But it didn't work that way. A lot of feminists might be horrified by his new pro-family approach, but a surprising number weren't at all upset by it.

He wasn't going to argue. Votes were votes. If the pseudo-dykes were willing to march with the Moral Majority that had recently come to understand the new personage that was Andrew Marston, then Andrew Marston wasn't going to scare them away.

"We have to move again. There has to be still more. More to justify the speech I'm giving in three days. It has to be spectacular." Marston was having a televised address at the convention center. His new coalition of his own personal crusade to save Minnesota morality was coming in from all over the state. They'd all be there to hear him, and all their friends would be at home glued to the television set.

This was the big jump-off point. Marston fully expected to pull off that most perfect political campaign, that one where to vote for him was to do the right thing; to oppose him was to do the wrong thing. Right and wrong; there would be no grey areas left by the time he was finished.

"More spectacular? Marston, are you crazy? We have implicated almost every rich closet-case fag in the Twin Cities for child molestation, sexual slavery, sadomasochism or something equally as *spectacular*. What more do you want?"

"I want more, I want much more. I want something that will dramatically underline the moral degradation that's taking over the country through the gay liberation movement. That kid, Anderson. I want him. And the dentist, Chisle, what's the deal? How the hell did he get out? I saw that on television."

"The federal attorney sprang him. The orders were from way up. *Way* up, they say. He'll still get his. I know he's still up for state charges ... "

Marston stopped Sonny LeBec's report. "No, no, I don't think Chisle should get his. I think we should show the good people of this state just what happens when a gay criminal is shown any justice."

Luther Angstrom was still playing with his letter opener. He was looking up, though, studying Marston. He seemed to understand. "A shame, a real shame, that a nice gay leader like that kid should have to pay the price for the liberal society's leniency."

"You got it," Marston said.

XIX

Martin Martello's cover was the Mar-Beth Importing exporting Company. It had taken its name from his and his wife's first names. Its offices were in a warehouse district in St. Paul, just over the border from Minneapolis on the long straight stretch of University Avenue that connected the two downtowns. The avenue was lined with department stores and shopping centers and small businesses like this one, housed in a single-story building of its own. The traffic on the street was dense, but now the cars and trucks were moving to and from the line of commercial enterprises; it no longer carried much of the inter-city traffic. I-95 did that nowadays.

His books looked awfully good. Getting those kids into the country and teaching them the ins and outs hadn't been cheap. But the pay-off was more than enough to justify the cost, he figured. At least in the long run it would be a good investment. It had to be. He had to get the state Attorney General off his back before the guy drove him crazy. Once Marston was in office . . .

"Hi."

Martin looked up. Two men were standing in the entry to his office. One of them scared him instantly. He was the kind of guy that Martin's girls talked about, the kind with a facial expression somewhere between insanity and rage. They were the dangerous ones, the ones that could turn on a girl with little notice if the wrong buttons were pushed.

His clothing was that kind of stuff that gay guys were always wearing. Button-fly jeans, black leather boots, a tight t-shirt. The shirt left his arms bare, bare enough that Martin knew the guy was strong. At first it didn't bother Martin; it was just like those gays to go and spend their spare time in a gym to build a body they'd never know how to use. All image and no substance. Why, if one of those guys ever came up against the hired hands that Martin had ...

"Wait a minute, how did you guys get in here?" Martello spent a lot of money on protection — a whole lot of money. The least that Martin could expect is that his own private office would be guarded by the goons he had on his payroll. But here were two gay guys who just walked in on him.

"Oh, we let your guards take a break. They're ... *resting.*" The other, younger guy seemed to think that was funny. He was chuckling as he spoke.

"I didn't tell those guys they could do that!"

"We sort of took the responsibility, Martello." The young guy was awfully good looking. Martin looked him over with an appraising eye. If he ever decided to move into guys, this is the kind he was sure would sell. Nice body — his chest seemed to be made in the shape of a V — and a good smile. Those little dimples were an extra attraction. Too bad his beard was so heavy. Even though the kid was clean shaven, there was the darkness of ... *Wait a minute!*

"What kind of business do you have here? I'm a busy man. I can't just spend my time with anyone who walks in off the street."

"You have plenty of time for us," the older guy said. "We want to talk about importing. You know about importing, that's what the sign says on your building. We've even heard a little about your successes. Seems you have some very fine merchandise that comes in from Guatemala. We want to talk about that."

Merchandise from Guatemala . . . ? Martin studied his intruders with a clearer eye. So they were interested in those kids that Martin had gotten for Marston's operation. The pair in front of him was obviously gay. There was no question now, Martello had put together the pieces of the puzzle. These guys were in the same business as himself, but they were doing it with the faggots. So they wanted some fresh Latin meat to peddle, did they? This could be interesting.

"Well, yes, let's talk about it." He swept a hand over the chairs that faced his desk. The men each took one and looked at him, obviously wanting him to take the lead.

"Well," Martin began, "it's not easy. After all, we're talking about shopping for the goods, getting the appropriate licenses, then a front organization that can deal with adoption papers and such here in this country; it all takes a great deal of money."

"Your wife comes in handy for all that, doesn't she?" Did that guy's eyes actually change color as he was talking?

"Hey, Beth is a pro. She can sniff out the best stuff and she has an uncanny way of knowing which is . . . more easily packaged."

"You mean, which boys will be the least difficult to manage?" the guy asked.

"Packaging these goods is a highly sophisticated business," Martin admitted. "Beth is just great at it."

"Where's Paco Rodriguez?"

"Who the hell's he?" Martin answered the young guy.

"The one you sold to Dr. Chisle. The one you made the police think Dr. Chisle bought."

"Hey, those kids are all in protective custody until the trial. I've helped arrange for the organization that got this all together to house them until — "

Before Martin could finish his sentence the older guy had

leapt across his desk and was dragging him to his feet with an iron grip on his necktie. *"I'm going to put you in protective custody of my own if you don't tell me where the fuck that kid is."*

Martin had gotten used to the guy's eyes, and he wasn't the sort of man to give in just because someone was yelling at him. But he somehow knew that this was not someone he wanted to fight with. The fact that these two had gotten past his guards flooded back into his mind. How had they done that? And what *was* it about this man . . .

"They're north of here, near St. Cloud. I'll draw you a map."

"You'll do better than that, asshole. You're going to give us a guided tour. Right now." With that Alex Kane began dragging Martin Martello out of his office and toward the building exit. "Burn the building, Danny. Light a fire. Fire's the only thing that can clean a place like this after vermin have taken over."

"A pleasure, Alex, a real pleasure."

Martin Martello was desperately trying to keep his consciousness as the guy dragged him out. But he did catch a look at Danny's face as the young man gathered together inflammable materials to begin the conflagration. There was something about his extraordinary anger that suddenly made Martin glad the Danny wasn't the one with the grip on his neck right now.

XX

Paco Rodriguez was scared and humiliated.

It had sounded like such a good idea when Señora Beth had come to his village high in the mountains of Guatemala. The well-dressed American lady had promised his mother that there would be great wealth if Paco would only take a vacation to America. He could receive an education here in the United States much better than any he had ever dreamed of in Guatemala.

Education!

He was sitting outside the shack they were housing him in, him and the others from the various countries around the Caribbean. They had all gone through the same thing. They had been taught that they would pose as servants and, some of them, adopted children in the homes of men here in this strange northern place called Minnesota.

Then they would only have to tell a few exaggerations in a court room. Some would be returned to their families with huge amounts of money. Others would be able to stay and go to American schools. They would only have to tell small lies.

Paco felt horrible about this. Dr. Allen hadn't been a bad men. Yes, he was a *maricon*. Paco had known that for sure when he'd found the glossy magazines with all the pictures of men in them. But he hadn't ever done to Paco what these men . . .

He squeezed his eyes shut to block out the memory. Dr. Allen had been good to him and he had paid him back with treachery. He had done a bad thing and he was going to have to repeat his lies again in another courtroom. All the man had done was ask Paco to work a little, then he'd taught the boy some English lessons and taken him to movies and bought him new clothes. All Paco had done in return was lie.

If he could regain his honor by telling the truth, he would gladly do it. Gladly. But he had no honor left to regain. He looked out over the area around the shack. There was nowhere to run. They had shown them that. Laughing, the guards had dared one boy, the black from Haiti, to try. He hadn't gotten more than a few hundred yards before the huge vicious dogs had caught him. Those beasts were always on patrol. They had told the boys that. If the guard hadn't blown his whistle when he had they all knew that the Haitian would be dead now.

He might as well be dead.

So might Paco. He had to endure, if only for his mother and his starving family in Guatemala. But what he had to do! What he had to do to stay alive and to keep the guards happy.

"Hey, spic-boy, come here."

Paco shuddered as he saw the worst of the guards standing nearby. Two of the big dogs knelt beside him. They were panting heavily, their ugly tongues hanging out and their saliva dripping down onto the ground.

Paco stood, shaking, and moved cautiously toward the guard. His name was Sam. Sam had a big belly, a huge stomach that hung out over the top of his belt. He wore dirty coveralls and had ugly teeth, teeth with big holes between them. He never seemed to have shaved. He always stank. He also always leered when he saw Paco.

He was groping his crotch long before the Guatemalan

youth reached him. Paco could see the all to familiar outline of the man's erection through his pants. "You spic-boys got great mouths, you know that. Man, I never had no broad could give head like you kids. Come on, I need a piece just about now. Come on, get down and take care of this 'fore the rest of them get back. Wouldn't do for one of them to see old Sam getting done by a spic-boy."

Paco closed his eyes. He'd dared refuse an order like this once before. The beating he'd received hadn't been too hard to take. What had been horrible had been the lecture he'd received from Señora Beth. The American lady had shown up the next day with pictures of Paco's family. She'd delivered her unmistakable warning then. They would pay for Paco's disobedience.

He had no doubt about the power of these strange Americans. There was no choice but to give in to them. Praying for forgiveness from the Madonna, Paco dropped to his knees. To do this to a nice man like Dr. Allen wouldn't have been so horrible. He would just have been thanking him for all the good things he'd received. But this pig-man! Paco's eyes were cast down. He heard the zipper opening. He could smell the foul odor that came from the man's unwashed crotch. "Got me a big load for you, spic-boy."

"I have a big load for you, too."

Paco and Sam turned their heads together at the same time. There was a man neither of them had ever seen before. He was only wearing jeans and a t-shirt. He had a look of great fury to him — the kind of fury that avenging angels had in the painting of the church in Paco's hometown.

"Get 'im." Sam ordered the big dogs into action. Paco averted his look. He had seen more than enough of the dogs' ability. He heard them attack. Their growling sent shivers through his body. Then there were a couple whines . . . and silence.

Paco was startled again. He turned to see what had happened. The dogs were still breathing, but they were sleeping at the man's feet, and the man's fury had not abated in the least.

The stranger moved toward Sam and Paco. He moved quickly. Sam tried to run, but he didn't have time. The man sank his fist into Sam's huge belly, his hand actually disappearing into the flabby mass. Sam's cheeks blew out from the impact of the blow. Another fist lashed out and smashed into Sam's face and Sam crumpled to the ground. His now flaccid penis was still hanging from his pants. Its tiny size looked ridiculous against the man's bulk.

"Stand up, son. You aren't spending any more time on your knees around here. Not ever again."

• • •

Paco had never seen the other boys so happy. The same man who had beaten up Sam, the one who called himself Alex Kane, had set a trap for the rest of the guards with the help of his friend, an American boy not much older than Paco. This youth, Danny, was friendly to them all. They all seemed to understand that Alex and Danny were both *maricones*, but they didn't care now. They were free, or at least they soon would be.

There were a dozen of them. They were all sitting at a MacDonald's eating their first meal of hamburger and fries in weeks. The Americans had even bought them all large colas.

The one called Danny asked them questions. He was writing in a small booklet with a pen. He was always smiling and friendly. The boy from Haiti, the one the others had supposed had enjoyed his adventures with the American *maricones*, seemed to be falling hopelessly in love with Danny as the black-haired young man wrote all the things that they said.

Paco seemed to be the only one to pay attention to a single detail. The hand that Danny used to grip the pen was white around the knuckles. He might be smiling at the boys, but inside, Paco knew, he was furious.

Paco sipped his cola and studied these two strange Americans. Somehow he knew they were going to salvage his honor. Somehow he knew.

XXI

Allen Chisle had a comfortable house near Lake Harriet, one of the nicer areas of Minneapolis. He could look out his front window and see the park that surrounded the lake. It was always a pleasure, but this time the water looked even more beautiful than ever.

"You're sure?" he asked Mike.

"Stop it, Allen, yes I'm sure." Mike was walking back into the front room with a beer in his hand. "I'm just sorry it's taken me so long to figure it out."

"Well, so long as . . . "

"Allen, stop being so calm and rational. Yes, I'm willing to move in with you. I love you. I want to stay with you. It's been difficult for me to deal with the age differences and the money issues. But I want to do it. I trust you totally now." Mike leaned over and kissed Chisle on the lips.

"I'll register at the University for this fall. There shouldn't be any problem. The social work people have been after me for a long time. I can at least start some courses and then move into the Master's program as soon as possible, as soon as the red tape allows.

"I need to move on. In a lot of ways. It's time to get some more academics going and it's time to get some more relationship going with you."

Allen was delirious with delight. After the nightmare they'd been going through, now there was more hope. There was something beautiful about it all. He'd always wanted to have someone like this, someone who he'd love to love. Here was Mike. Here was his happiness.

The two men stood and embraced each other. Their lips meshed nicely. Their arms went around each other's chest. They were so happy they didn't hear the door open.

"Pretty picture."

They froze, then quickly broke their posture and turned to look toward the intruding voice. There were three men standing in the living room. All three had revolvers in their hands.

"Hey, Luther, let's make it prettier," one of them joked.

"We're going to make it a lot prettier," Luther smiled.

• • •

Luther Angstrom had enjoyed the gang war that had won him absolute control of the Upper Midwest drug trade. The bodies that littered rural Minnesota had been a kind of job to him. They had taken him back to some forgotten pleasures of his youth.

Luther had always been the kind of kid who loved to pull wings off of living butterflies. He had enjoyed putting out cigarettes on young kittens. When he's played doctor with the little girls in his neighborhood, he'd seldom been willing to stop with explorations. The girl didn't squirm enough if you only "explored." He was equally happy when he was playing cowboy and Indians with the other boys. Then there was an excuse to tie them up. He especially had liked playing cowboys since he had declared that the rules made it necessary for Indians to be whipped. Luther had demanded that the games be played with great authenticity.

Now the drug czar stood at the foot of Allen Chisle's big double bed. He was grinning at the new stimuli that were rekindling his favorite childhood thoughts. There, spreadeagled and bound to the four posts, was the naked squirming body of Mike Anderson. The kid had a nearly hairless body, typical of blonds and in itself boyish enough to fire Luther's thoughts.

He should be squirming. He was looking at the little arsenal of toys that Luther had brought along.

"Hey, Luther, can't we just off the guy? This is going to be messy this way."

"No," Luther answered curtly. "We have to do it right. We have to make it look like the other one, the dentist, did it. It's gotta look like the kid was enjoying himself and being enjoyed by the other guy. Remember how we did that? You just pump a load of lead into him and it's too simple a murder."

Luther sat down on a chair in the corner. This was going to take a while. Besides, sitting down, Luther could cross his legs and hide the erection he was popping. It wouldn't do any good to have the boys see the boss throwing a rod over a young guy.

Luther's right hand man, Frank, shrugged. Luther paid him a damn good salary. If Luther wanted it, Luther would have what he wanted. Frank took off his sports jacket and unbuttoned the sleeves of his shirt. He rolled them up his arms till they were over his elbows.

He looked at the mess of equipment that Luther had brought, then finally lifted up a lethal-looking cat of nine tails. The leather strands hung from a single grip. "This do the trick?"

"Sure," Luther said. "But start at the ends, his chest, his legs. It's gotta look like they did it for a long time."

"Let me show you what he means." Alex Kane had appeared out of nowhere. He stalked across the room before anyone could react. When Luther finally reached for the gun he had replaced in his shoulder holster he froze. A cold piece of metal was against his forehead.

"I don't think you want to reach in there," a voice said.

Very cautiously Luther looked up and saw a young guy standing there holding the gun. The kid had dimples, for Christ's sake! But with that gun right at Luther's head, the gangster wasn't going to hand out compliments on dimples right now.

Alex Kane had first retrieved the guns from Frank and the other hired hand. He threw them out the open window he had entered through. The two men moved back into the corner; whoever this guy was, they didn't want to tangle with him. Besides, there was the other one with a gun at their boss's head. They couldn't take any chances with the boss's life, or so they rationalized.

Next Alex picked up the horrible looking whip and brandished it about. He came over to Luther Angstrom and smiled. Then, with one quick movement that gave Luther no warning, he reached back and brought the whip slashing across the dope peddler's face. Bright tracks of blood glistened in the whip's trail.

"Isn't that how it works?" Alex Kane asked.

XXII

Sonny LeBec loved to count his money. He knew that he should just let the accountants do it. But every once in a while he loved getting his own hands on his own cash. It didn't matter to him that the stuff was soaked with beer, faded from the constant handling in one of his gay bars. It was real money — real cash that showed just how great a success he was. He was a very real success according to the piles of dough that he had piled up in front of him.

"*Boss!*" his manager yelled. Sonny looked up; Bruno should know better than to interrupt him at this greatest of pleasures. "Boss, they got Luther. He talked. It was on the radio. He mentioned you. Martello too. They got him. He's spilling the beans about everything."

"Everything?" Sonny couldn't believe his ears.

"Everything about you. Nothing about Marston."

Sonny did some quick calculations. It would make sense. That's what he'd do. If they got him involved in all this shit he could have his ass in federal pens for the rest of his life. His one hope would be a friend like Marston in the governor's chair making some deals with Washington. Marston would have to do it, too. He'd *have* to.

But Sonny wasn't about to take any risk like that. What could ever have happened to make a hardass like Luther Angstrom talk? That man was the kind that made everyone else quake, the way he played with his letter openers and the way . . .

No, not now. Sonny looked at the pile of money on his desk. There were thousands in cold cash here. More thousands in the safe. There were the bank accounts in Vegas and bigger ones in Switzerland. Sonny had always planned on having his options kept open, just in case.

This was definitely sounding like a time to exercise those options. Definitely. "Come on, Bruno, we're going to have a little vacation in Vegas. It's getting hot around here."

"But, boss, Nevada's even hotter."

Sonny looked at the over-muscled goon and sighed. Bruno never was one for brains. "Let's just get packed up." Bruno followed orders as Sonny brought out traveling cases and explained how Bruno should pack them with the loose money.

They had cleaned out the counting room and were on their way to Sonny's car. *Jesus, what could make Luther Angstrom talk?* Sonny was hurrying down the alleyway. There would be a very early flight west, it was already approaching dawn now. They could take anything available, to LA, Reno, Denver, Sonny didn't care. It just sounded as though it was a good time to get out of Minnesota.

He was thinking so hard he ran right into the man, hitting his head against a shockingly hard chest. Sonny was stunned. "Get the fuck out of my way."

The man smiled, and when he did his eyes seemed to light up into an awesome green. "You heard the boss, move." Bruno loyally stepped forward and pushed an arm against the man. He didn't budge.

"Don't hurt my friend," a voice warned.

Bruno and Sonny looked over to see where the words came from. A young guy with dimples was standing there with his arms crossed over his front. Bruno and Sonny smiled. A kid telling a pro like Bruno what to do. "You gonna stop me?" Bruno was having a good time now. He reached out to shove the strange looking man once more.

The other one just shook his head, as though in some kind of mock disappointment. "I told you so." Sonny watched as the kid seemed to take his mark, like he was going to run a race or something, he was standing a way Sonny had seen before. Oh, yeah, in the Olympics, when those gymnastic guys were getting ready to do their tricks.

This kid was just like them. Then he began to move, and once he did Sonny had a hard time keeping his eyes on the kid's movements. He was racing across the alley one second and then, unbelievably, he was airborn. *Just like the fucking Olympics.*

The kid did some kind of somersault in the air and it was just fucking beautiful to watch. For everyone but Bruno. Because when the kid came down from his leaping somersault — he must have twirled around three times up there! — his boots landed squarely on Bruno's jaw. The huge man collapsed into a heap — he was out cold.

Sonny was very impressed — so impressed that when the kid told him to put down his bags and follow them, Sonny did *not* have a moment's hesitation in complying with his request. Not one.

"How did you do that?" Sonny finally asked.

Danny smiled. "It's just something you learn." Then he put an arm around Alex Kane's waist.

XXIII

Tim Ranson's doorbell rang. He didn't want to answer it. He hadn't had a shower in a couple days. His clothes were dirty. He was working on a bottle of Vodka and he didn't want any company except the welcome relief of the booze. But the bell kept going.

"Oh, shit." Tim gave up and walked over to answer it. "You." The last person in the world he wanted to see was Mike Ahern. "Go fuck yourself."

Tim slammed the door shut and went back to his drink. He toasted himself. He'd wanted to do that for a long time. A long, long time. The buzzer sounded again. "Fucker can't take a hint."

Tim unsteadily got up and walked over to the door again. "I don't want to talk to you," he screamed at Ahern. "I don't want anything to do with you."

Mike walked in and took the bottle out of Tim's hand. The pilot tried to grab it back, but he was too blasted. "Come on, Tim. You look in pretty bad shape. Let's stop this for a — "

"I don't know what the fuck you're doing, but I don't need any help from a fucking breeder right now. I'd like to be left alone."

Mike hesitated. He bit his lip. "I deserve that."

"You're fucking right you do. You fucking asshole. It's

your fault and all the others. I don't want shit from you." He made another attempt to retrieve the bottle. Mike wasn't ready to give in.

"Let's talk."

"Talk? Talk about what? Faggots and cocksuckers? Gangsters and pimps? Is that what you want to talk about? Lives ruined and men going unpunished? Is that what you—"

Mike reared back and sent a harsh slap against Tim's face. It was a hard enough blow that Tim went sprawling over the carpet. "Shut up! We're going to get your act together before this goes any further."

Tim ran a hand across his mouth. He could taste his own blood. He wanted to stand up and get even, but Mike had moved too quickly. He was dragging Tim into the bathroom. "I'm not sure what's the biggest mess, you or this place," Mike scowled. Tim couldn't resist when Mike began undressing him after having started the shower running.

"I'll . . . I'll do it myself."

"Can you manage?" Mike demanded.

"Yes." Tim could — barely. He climbed into the shower after he'd undressed. The water felt good, warm and comforting. There hadn't been many things that had been warm and comforting lately. Not at all. Nothing had been. He let himself go, just enjoying the almost strange sensation of becoming clean.

It was a long shower. His skin was actually puckered by the time he was done. He was a little more sober now. He looked in the mirror and saw the devastation of the past few weeks. The least he could do was shave; he reached into the medicine cabinet and brought out an electric razor, then ran it over his face.

He left his dirty clothes on the floor when he was finished. He put a towel around his waist and went into the kitchen. Mike had been cleaning up. The old newspapers and the dirty dishes were already gone and he was scrubbing the sink with cleanser now.

"What the hell are you doing?"

"I'm helping out a friend here who obviously doesn't know how to clean up after himself."

"Why you? Why here? Why now?"

Mike didn't stop cleaning. "I've heard the stories, Tim. All of them. I know what happened. I know how it happened."

"Yeah," Tim wasn't sure he wanted to go through this right now.

"Yeah. It was his closet, wasn't it?"

Tim nodded.

"They say that what happened was they went to him and told him that if he didn't put out they were going to go to his law firm, right?"

"Yes."

"So he thought they just wanted a piece of his ass. Was he that good looking?"

"Yes."

"So, rather than fight back or tell them to fuck themselves, he let them do what they wanted to?"

"They started with one of the bartenders that LeBec had under his control, so it looked sort of real. You know, it was guy who worked at a gay bar. He just told Ralph that he had to play along. They had pictures of us on vacation in Provincetown and they'd show them to—"

"So, Ralph gave in. Then the gangsters who were for real moved in, right? That Angstrom guy that's in all the papers?"

"Yes."

"That's what I heard." Mike had rinsed off the sink. He moved on to find a bucket under the cabinet. He filled it with detergent and water, then retrieved a mop and began to wash the tiles on the kitchen floor. "There's a lesson there. It's a hard one for you to even think about. But it's one I have to learn."

"What?"

"Closets kill."

Tim watched as his co-pilot kept scrubbing. There was sweat running down Ahern's forehead. But then Tim realized it wasn't just sweat, there were tears.

"Do you mean . . ."

"I always thought I could keep it secret. It's why I badgered you so much. Hell, I spent the whole time in that cockpit furious with you. I knew about Ralph. Everyone at Farmdale Industries knew about Ralph. It didn't make any difference to anyone else. But it sure as hell made a difference to me. It was something forbidden. Something I couldn't have. I thought I couldn't have.

"I hated you and I hated the thought of him. I was making do with a couple blowjobs in tea rooms and you were living together. You had everything I wanted and thought I couldn't get. I was so damned worried about my reputation and what people would think. Every time I heard them make a joke about you — didn't happen often, but it did happen — it was like they were talking about me.

"I should have gotten pissed off, I suppose, but instead I just moved in deeper. I didn't want them talking about me that way. I didn't want people to . . .

"When I heard about Ralph and you, I even thought that was more reason. He died because of it. Then I realized I'd died a long time ago. I hadn't had any life in years. All my money and all my time was spent perfecting my facade.

"You know what I wanted all that time?"

"What?" Tim asked.

"I always wanted to know a man well enough to wash his floors for him."

With that, Mike started mopping with renewed vigor and a huge laugh.

• • •

When Tim woke up the next day his hangover was worse

than usual. He realized it was because he'd stopped drinking. He had learned a secret earlier: that if you just drank constantly you didn't get hangovers, you were always too drunk to have one.

He slowly got out of bed and reached for his robe. He made his way into the living area of his new small apartment. There was coffee perking; the odor was surprisingly seductive. He could hardly wait. He sprawled on a chair and took stock of things.

Coffee already brewing!

He suddenly came to full consciousness. His apartment was spotless, absolutely, perfectly clean. The windows were washed, the woodwork shined, the floors had been polished. Mike Ahern came out of the bathroom just then. "Slept on your couch, hope you don't mind."

The co-pilot walked over to the kitchen counter and saw that the coffee was nearly done. He got two mugs out and then poured them full of coffee. "Black?"

"Fine," Tim mumbled.

Ahern was clad only in his jockey shorts. Tim had never even thought of the guy as anything but an enemy before. He certainly hadn't thought of him sexually. But now, seeing Ahern in a state of near undress with only the clinging cotton fabric to cover him, Tim had to acknowledge that he was a pretty well-built man.

Tim took the coffee and sipped the scalding hot liquid. "Thanks."

Mike sat down with his legs spread. He had the masculinity of a jock. It hadn't been just Tim's misimpression that led him to think of Ahern as a straight man. Few gay men sat like that naturally, with their legs open and the clearly visible pouch of their jockey shorts open to . . .

Tim did a quick double take of his emotions. *Oh, no.* "Look, Mike, I don't really know what's up here. But I gotta tell you that I'm not ready for it. I mean, just because you think that you want . . ."

"There's nothing up. You're someone who should have been my friend a long time ago. I just want to help a bit. So I got compulsive about cleaning. I think best when I'm doing things like that. So, I slept on your couch. I did sleep on your *couch*. You need a friend, Tim, there's no way you can deny it. You need someone to keep you from this solitary misery of yours. I need a friend, too. I need a friend badly."

"It's not just you, it's the . . . the memory."

"I respect that memory. Honestly, I do. It's a hard time for both of us. I . . . I'm not in practice about this stuff, being a good friend and helping out emotionally. But if you'll let me, I'll sure as hell try, Tim. I mean that. I'll sure as hell try."

A friend sounded pretty good right now. Tim nodded.

"Hey, look, I don't have to work today. Want to go see the Twins? They're playing."

"The Twins? Mike, I am *not* going to go out and make believe I'm some straight guy going to a fucking ball game."

"Do you like baseball?"

"Yes, but . . . "

"So we'll do a little shopping first."

• • •

That afternoon two men, both in their thirties, walking with big smiles on their faces, climbed into box seats to watch the Minnesota Twins play baseball. If they heard any remarks about their t-shirts which had "Gay and Proud" across them in bold lettering, they didn't seem to notice.

• • •

Two weeks later they were back in Tim's apartment again. "Don't you think it's time you did something besides babysit me?" Tim asked.

"What do you mean?" As always, Mike Ahern was cleaning.

"Mike, you've spent nearly every day with me. What about your job? What about doing something on your own? I feel like ..."

"You know perfectly well that Farmdale Industries gives all kinds of benefits. There are personal days, there are days you can save up from vacation, all that. I just took them. Actually, I think it's more important for you to go back to work. You're in good shape now, Tim. Come on, let's start flying again."

Tim looked at Ahern. Mike was right. Besides, the prospect of spending time at work with his co-pilot was full of utterly new possibilities now. Mike had grown a moustache. After studying photographs in *Mandate*, he'd gone and had a new, short clone-style haircut. He also had quickly accumulated an imposing collection of t-shirts.

"Yeah, it's time."

• • •

Farmdale Industries had subsidiaries all over the United States. The company's planes were often loaned out to various charities as well; the pilots who flew their private fleet could be sent anywhere. But since the old man lived in California and since New York was the center of the financial world, those two were the most usual destinations.

The first assignment Tim and Mike had was to ferry some equipment from Minneapolis to the San Francisco area. It was easy to arrange a stopover. Mike was particularly delighted. "Show me the spots, Tim, come on. Do you realize I've only been in two gay bars in my life and they were in Duluth and Fargo?"

Tim smiled. He figured he owed that much to Mike. They did Castro Street first. Mike acted as though he were in Disneyland. The gymnasium-perfect bodies paraded up and down the thoroughfare in various stages of undress, their owners' bodies and sexual possibilities clearly apparent.

It was a difficult thing to introduce Mike to everything at once. There were the handkerchiefs to explain and the leather icons as well. When they walked into an S&M bar Tim had a rush of sadness and discomfort. He didn't want to stay there, not after what had happened to Ralph. They moved on and ate dinner at a gay restaurant on Market Street.

"Does he really want me that badly?"

Tim laughed, "Yes, he wants you that badly." A cute waiter had all but thrown himself on Mike's lap.

"But I'm older than he is by ten years. He's the one with the body."

"Well, the ten years is probably want he wants. It's a daddy trip."

"Daddy trip? Hell, I'd just want to wax his linoleum." They both laughed at that.

"And you have a perfectly fine body." Tim blushed as he said that. The thought had been going through his mind since the first time he'd seen Mike in his underwear that day. But he didn't . . .

Mike seemed equally uncomfortable."Well, let's get our check cleared up and then get out of here. I want to go to some more bars."

"Oh, Mike, really?" There was a sharpness in Tim's voice. He immediately regretted it.

"No, we can go back to the room if you're tired. Or, if you wanted to just go on by yourself, well, I guess I've taken up a lot of your time. I mean, you're probably horny and want to go and get your rocks off. I guess I'm just not used to all these things yet and I should have—"

"*Stop it!*" Tim's command was quick and harsh. He took a deep breath. "That's not what I meant. Look, we're supposed to be honest, right? Okay. The reason I don't want to do bars any more is that I'm sick and tired of watching you and half the men of San Francisco cruising each other. Not because I don't like looking at you or them, but because . . . I'm jealous. What I really want to do is take you back to the hotel room and fuck the brains out of you."

Mike sat back in chair, stunned. Tim thought he'd really

blown the whole thing this time. *What a jerk I am.*

"Well . . ." Mike stuttered, "that'd be great. If you leave enough grey cells so I can still fly a plane and wash a dish, that is."

• • •

The first time.

They were so tentative. They were a little frightened of each other, not frightened of rejection or pain, but because they didn't know the secrets yet, the places that hurt, the places that gave great pleasure.

They were in the hotel room and began undressing. *We're going to do it.* They were both in awe of that fact. They were not just watching another man strip; they were watching the revelation of a gift they were going to receive. When their shoes, socks and shirts were removed, they moved close to one another. They embraced.

The little electric shock started when they felt chest hair against chest hair. They could each smell the other's odor as their arms were lifted, and the musky aroma goaded them on. Hands moved over backs, feeling muscle and prodding flesh. They could feel each other's hardness as two erections fought for escape from the confines of their pants.

But most of all, there were the kisses, the saliva moving together, the tongues rolling wetly off one another; those explorations were the symbol for all the intruding and all the submitting that was to follow.

It was Mike who couldn't wait. Mike who had been waiting for too long. Mike who pulled back and looked longingly into Tim's eyes. Then he fell to his knees. He wasn't just undoing a zipper when his hands moved against Tim's fly. He was beginning an adventure. One that, somehow, they both knew would go on and on and on . . .

He finished, leaned forward and pressed his head against the bulge there, the restraining cotton of Tim's underwear acting as a tease to both of them. Mike opened his mouth and ran it along the hard shaft.

He kept at it until there was a moan too real from Tim's mouth over him. Only then did Mike reach in and release the hard cock. It sprang forward, a tiny hint of wetness at its tip.

The first time.

Mike looked at it with obvious delight and quickly took it all in. For the first time, he finally had that longed-for erection in his mouth. He worked it, moving up and down, sucking on it, desperate to give it as much pleasure as he was receiving himself.

Tim finally pushed him back, not willing to go over the edge into orgasm yet. Kneeling on the floor, looking up at this other man's face as his cheek was being caressed with tender care, Mike felt an overwhelming sensation. *This is what it's like when someone looks at you with love.*

They finished undressing and moved to the bed. For so many years Mike had been so closed, his secrets entrapping him in his guilt and his self-protection. Now, with the memory of Tim's expression, he wanted to shatter that whole series of buffers. "Fuck me, please. Fuck me." He whispered the words as he clung to Tim with a pressure that let his pilot know just how important this was.

Tim had a lubricant in his bag. He got it and greased himself. An oily finger moved into the private entrance to Mike's body. A groan came from the co-pilot. It was half surrender and half victory, both merged together. "Yes."

Tim moved on top of Mike, spreading the other man's legs apart and lifting them. He pressed: there was resistance, then there was none. There was nothing but the undeniable and total pleasure of feeling his cock encased in this man's ass.

The movements were slow, as though both men wanted to linger at this place for as long as possible. But the pent-up passion and frustration wouldn't allow it. Tim began to move faster and faster. Mike did nothing to slow him down, he gripped Tim's hips and pulled — sometimes savagely. He wanted these defenses destroyed, absolutely destroyed.

There was a sudden tightening of Tim's body. Spasms shook his whole being, a cry came from his throat, a guttural roar. Then he collapsed on Mike's body. The two men were panting. Their breath took a while to slow to a more manageable level. Only then did Tim realize that they were being glued together with a fluid beside their sweat.

"You came? That way?"

"Oh yeah."

They kissed. *The first time.* Without speaking they knew this one was going to last.

• • •

It was a couple months later. They had moved again, this time to a larger place. A house, actually. Tim had always wanted to own his own house, but he and Ralph had decided that their schedules wouldn't allow them to keep one up.

Mike and Tim's schedules didn't really give them that kind of time either, but Tim could count on Mike's unending energy. The idea that there was a whole structure that belonged to them, themselves, was too much to allow him to sit still. Mike continually assured Tim that the workload he carried didn't have to be matched. "Just let me run free."

"Running free" meant: cleaning, washing, ironing, painting, scraping, polishing, refinishing, refurbishing, re...

"You make me tired just watching you," Tim finally complained. *"Please,* have a beer and let's just watch some television."

"I know, I know I'm boring about it all. Okay, I'll do that." Mike had on his Christopher Street t-shirt, a new purchase they'd made on a recent trip to New York. "Can we go to Fire Island next summer," he suggested as he sat down.

"We probably should. There or Provincetown."

"You agree then? I figure I need the exposure, you know, to that kind of summer gay life."

"I figure you need to go to a place where there's going to be a constant supply of sand being tracked around to keep you happy as you clean it up."

They laughed and kissed and Mike finally made himself put his feet up on the table as the news came on. "That's him, isn't it?"

Andrew Marston was being interviewed.

"Our next governor." Tim took an angry drink at his can of beer.

"How did it happen?" Mike asked. "How could a crook like that not only get away, but put himself on the road to the state mansion? I mean ..."

"It happened because the others won't talk. They got caught, they're in prison. They think this guy's going to become governor and then they'll get pardoned. All the squealing they did on one another was one thing. They just weren't going to get rid of their one shot at freedom."

"But that guy Mike Anderson said that it *was* him."

"It was. We know it. But no one's going to believe us. Besides, you've watched how he's side-stepped the issues. He made himself seem to be the one who brought about the capture of all those others. It was his moral crusade that set them up."

"Who can believe that shit after what he had said about gays?"

"Anybody. Saying stupid things about gays isn't going to lose anyone any credibility. You should have learned that by now."

"I can't believe it. Anderson told me about that pair of guys who took care of everyone. Why couldn't they have handled Marston, too?"

"Because, if they did anything to the leader of the moral crusade in Minnesota, it'd just fire up all the right wing crazies and we'd be in worse trouble. There's nothing to do." Tim put down his can and sat back on the couch, his arms crossed against his chest in a sulk.

Mike wouldn't drop it. He knew he couldn't. The life he and Tim were putting together was a good one, a fine one. But it had a shadow, one that could blot them out. The memory of Ralph and what had been done to him was too painful, it was baggage that even a relationship as good as theirs couldn't handle.

"He should be punished," Tim announced.

"It would have to be God or nature that interfered. Hell, if anyone laid a finger on his holy body we'd have a crusade going that wouldn't ever be stopped."

"He should be punished." *And I think I know how to do it.*

• • •

Later that night, when Tim had already gone to bed, Mike decided to make a phone call. If he was right there was something that could be done.

He had had enough conversations with Mike Anderson about the events in Minnesota to understand that the two strangers had been involved in the clean up of the anti-gay forces in the Twin Cities. They had a lot to do with it.

You don't just have white slavers like Martin Martello who've lived off children give themselves up to the police. Drug dealers who have existed outside the law don't get caught with as much evidence as that Angstrom guy had had on him without someone pulling something. All of it, the dirty bar business, the pushers, the murder, all of it stopped all at once. Everyone had been sentenced to jail and the best lawyers in the city weren't going to get them out of it.

Mike had put together his conversations with Anderson and his own observations of things. There were certainly something that could be done about Marston. Mike figured he knew a way to handle it, and that way needed some help from a friend in California. He dialed the number and listened to the phone ring at the other end.

XXIV

Paco and his Haitian friend, Jean-Luc, splashed happily in the New Hampshire lake. The four adult men watched from the shore.

"The kids sure are happy," Allen Chisle said. "It's great having them around."

"How is he adjusting to you and Mike? And you to him? I mean, I'm not sure I'd want a budding heterosexual like that living with me." Danny had heard all about Paco's precocious straight sexuality.

"Well, it's fine. Really it is. I guess I wouldn't have taken a straight kid normally, but we figured he had some responsibility. He was caught in the net with the rest of them." Allen Chisle sipped his cola.

"But Jean-Luc *is* gay. Is Paco giving him grief?"

"No, no," Mike Anderson assured Danny "They're like guys who've been through combat together. There's a bond that can't be broken. They're the best of friends, you should hear them brag to each other. They do fight, but it's only over who has the better looking friend. What sex that 'friend' is doesn't seem the issue."

"It's good having them. I think it's good that the whole community has all those kids. There were twenty-five of them in all. It was a raw deal. It would have been an even worse thing to send them all back to their home countries without any of the things they had been promised. Now they're getting their educations and their futures. It's taken a lot of work and fundraising, but all the kids that were lured up to the states are getting what was promised to them.

"It sure has changed gay Minneapolis, though," Allen continued. "I mean, everyone seems to have an adopted teenage son these days. We go to more kid parties than anything else."

"Like this," Mike indicated the kids who were still squealing with delight. "We really appreciate your inviting us. But we couldn't have come without them."

"No problem," Alex said. "None at all."

"I'm not sure about Mr. Farmdale though. Do you think he'll mind that we're bringing these two to dinner with us? He's so intimidating to me. I just don't see him enjoying dinner with a couple youngsters."

Alex Kane seemed to be delighted with the prospect. "No problem."

• • •

"This is one of the finest and most proper eating establishments in New England." Joseph Farmdale was literally glowering. "How could you bring those hellions here?"

They were in the lobby of the Red Crow Inn. Farmdale had lured Alex away from the table, but Alex stood his ground. "It's your own fault."

"My own fault! How could you say that?!"

"You're the one who pulled all the strings in Washington. If it weren't for you, they'd all be back in their home countries right now."

"In dire poverty, after having been misused by those filthy gangsters. Why, those gay men were desperate to make it up to the boys. After what they'd been through, the way they'd been blackmailed..."

"Especially Jean-Luc; after all, he's gay. Black and beautiful and gay."

"Don't you *dare* throw that at me! You know perfectly well that I do not condone any kind of racial prejudice. Now, this is one issue, but what's going on in that dining room is quite another issue. I mean, really, Alex. Those children..."

"Are your guests."

"You told me there would be houseguests of yours. But..."

"They are my houseguests. Now look, Farmdale. There's no way around it. You wanted to help. You did."

"But children would be best off in nurseries until they've learned their table manners. Those two..."

• • •

"Yuck, look at all that stuff on the meat," Paco said. "What is it?"

"It is a perfectly accomplished sauce in the finest traditions of—" Farmdale paled as he watched Paco scrape the sauce off his New York steak.

"I don't like sauce."

"Me either." Jean-Luc peeled the skin off his chicken l'orange to remove the offending liquid.

"Without those sauces, this food becomes something that you could have been served..."

"Why didn't we go to McDonald's? We love McDonald's."

"Don't whine, Paco. Mr. Farmdale's being very generous with you."

"*McDonald's!*" The sound that came from Joseph Farmdale's throat wasn't just a yell. It carried with it a great, intolerable pain, the pain of a man of tradition watching the emergence of modern day life at a closer view than he had ever been forced to witness it before. *"McDonald's."* The second time he spoke the name, it sounded more like a cry of grief.

Alex Kane was enjoying himself immensely.

• • •

The next day it seemed as though Alex had understood that the night at the Red Crow had taken Farmdale too far. He called the inn and told the old man to come to the house for dinner. Only when he was promised that the boys would be restrained in some way did Farmdale accept.

The five men were sitting drinking some of Farmdale's favorite vintage St. Emilion. Off across the lawn Jean-Luc and Paco were happily eating hamburgers while, on the grill, the adults' venison steaks were grilling. There was a decent salad that Danny had already prepared to accompany the game, and potatoes baking in the grill's coals.

"This will do very well."

Farmdale was obviously pleased. Danny reached over and filled his glass with wine. "Yes, indeed, my doctors need never know about this."

"Is that why you've come all the way to New Hampshire?" Mike asked.

Danny was the one to express pleasure this time. "No, he comes pretty regularly now. To visit family."

"Oh, do you have relatives near by?" Mike was innocently pursuing this topic. He didn't understand why both Farmdale and Alex Kane looked away with such theatrical distaste.

"The closest," Danny beamed.

"Well, you and your family have certainly been most generous to us, Mr. Farmdale. I mean, the contribution you made to the gay adoption fund will certainly go a long way in helping us out. I can afford the extra expense of two kids, but some of the guys just wouldn't have made it without your help."

Farmdale seemed pained by Allen's exposure of his generosity. Alex Kane moved in for an attack. "Can't keep your hands out of other people's business, can you? You had to go and spread all your money around again, didn't you?"

"You will never know how much money I have spent on your latest adventure, and its repercussions. You will never know."

XXV

Andrew Marston could not believe his good fortune. He'd made it! He had honestly and truly made it. He'd pulled off a change in his moral crusade after it had been a change of direction himself. The events in Minnesota had been a whirlwind of confusion and unbelievable contradictions.

But he'd ridden out the storm. He had proven his mettle in this baby, that's for sure.

All those assholes were in prison. They hadn't a shred of evidence to implicate him. It'd be a couple of years before they would realize they were never going to be pardoned. Angstrom, LeBec and the whole gang were gone. Sure, they'd make noise when they realized the extent of his double-cross. But he would have had time to bring together his resources and fill the vacuum. He'd be in charge of the above-board power of the state and also the underground power of crime.

He looked out his window and watched the Minnesota landscape racing by beneath him. His own state. The whole thing was going to be his.

He was deliciously pleased as he sipped his Scotch. He was thinking about the details. Another year and he could get a divorce. He'd be governor by then and it would give him and the electorate four years to forget that problem. He would marry any one of a number of women then. Women were always attracted to a powerful man. He could already see himself on the cover of *Time*. The television cameras followed him constantly. He was a celebrity.

Even his means of transportation proved it. Here he was in his private jet. Leased, granted, but it was his own. The deal had been great. So great he wondered about it until the salesman had explained that the company, a newly formed subsidiary of Farmdale Industries, needed the exposure of a star like himself to make it more credible in the marketplace. So they'd given Marston a deal.

That made sense. He's heard about all the women who got designer dresses and furs just so the creators would get the publicity that came with those well-known women wearing their clothes. This firm was just making a gamble, a gamble that made sense to Marston. They'd use his name in their advertising once they knew that Marston had won his election.

Scratch my back, I'll scratch yours, Marston smiled. There were lots of possibilities about being a governor of a state.

He looked up as the co-pilot came back into the executive lounge. Marston was the only passenger on this trip, a quick jaunt up to Thief River Falls. This two-man crew the company provided was a little weird. They seemed to always be studying Marston. They probably just had never been this close to someone as important as he before.

"Enjoying your journey?"

"Very much." Marston put on his best campaign smile.

"It's going to be a very important one for you."

"Yes, yes, any time I can get a chance to address a group of loyal Minnesota voters is very important." What a bunch of crap this guy was pulling.

Just then the pilot joined them. *Both of them...*

Then Marston saw the gun. "Don't bother moving." Mike held the pistol on Marston while Tim got the ropes.

The pilot secured Marston to his seat with quick and effective knots. "They don't have to be all that good. I made sure of his record. He can't fly. Not that it matters."

"What are you doing?"

Marston was panicking as he watched the two men put on parachutes. "We're climbing good now," the co-pilot said to the other. "This is more than high enough." They went toward the door.

"The plane's on automatic pilot. It'll keep in its path for quite a while, going directly toward Thief River Falls. No one will know the difference. It will climb, but not so much that you'll lose consciousness, we just wanted to get high enough to jump. You'll be wide awake when it happens. You'll hear first one engine sputter then the other. Then you'll feel the plane lose altitude. The plane's fall will accelerate quickly. Very quickly. You'll be able to feel that.

"We hope you enjoy this trip, Marston. You've got about an hour. An hour tops. You can think about it all. Think about the men you killed and the lives you ruined. We want you to do that.

"You can struggle if you want. Don't bother. Just in case you decided to play hero or got smart, I smashed the radio up. More insurance," Mike held up a handful of small electronic items. "The plane's not going anywhere we wouldn't want it to without these.

"Enjoy your hour, Marston. And think. Think a lot."

Then the two men opened the rear door, took each other's hand, and jumped.

Frantic, Marston turned until he could look out the window and see their parachutes loosen. They were drifting toward land. And he was drifting toward . . .

XXVI

The two figures were dressed in the traditional *gi*. Their martial arts costume seemed splendidly chosen for their flowing motions. They were practicing tai chi, the most graceful of the arts.

In liquid moves, their bodies moved in perfect synchrony. An arm mirrored an arm; leg a leg. The breeze of the early autumn in New Hampshire moved with them, complimenting them. Theirs was a ballet of physical perfection, a symbol of total companionship.

They kept at it for an hour as the dawning sun warmed the cool mountain air. They were unaware of any discomfort. They only were aware of one another and their two bodies.

When they finished, they gave the expected bow to one another. But then the taller, older of the two did the unexpected. He moved to his partner. First he removed his own *gi*. Then, reverently, he took off the other man's. When they were both naked, he fell to his knees. He placed both his hands under the testicles of the standing figure and seemed to cup them, as though they were a vessel of great value.

He leaned forward. His tongue came out and he ran it over the hair-covered surface, as though giving honor to the sweat that had come from their joint exertion. Only after he'd done his honor to all of that surface did he take in the swollen penis. His moves now were no faster than those earlier ones.

This was a quiet passion. It was the passion of a man who knew that his lover was not going to leave him. Not for a long, long time.

When they both were spent, when each had taken the fluids of the other, they moved to the lake. Its waters were already chilled in preparation for winter. They dove in without hesitation.

When they came out their skin was ruffled with evidence of the cold. They embraced still again, as though they had cooled themselves so much only to be able to have the joy of giving each other more warmth.

Then, naked and pleased, they walked up to their log cabin home and went about making their meal.

• • •

That night, as they sat and read in front of the fire that roared with large dry logs, Alex Kane was aware of the peace of his lover and himself. "Danny," he softly interrupted the younger man's quiet. "We can just stay here."

Danny waved the objections away. "We've been through all that. We'll spend the time we can together here. And when we have to leave..."

Alex went back to his novel. He was uncomfortable.

Danny's involvement made him look at his own so much. Was he addicted to all this? Was this something that he could do with another person? Could he lead this life with another man — who could suffer the consequences?

There was a knock on the door. It was nearly ten o'clock. It could only mean...

Danny had gotten up and answered the summons. There was a messenger there. He handed Danny a package, then left. The two lovers looked at one another. They knew.

Danny went over to the fire and opened the parcel. He threw away the wrappings. But he kept the contents.

It was a book, a red leather book, bound in the finest old Spanish tradition.